MW01115814

Cara Wylde was born in Romania and grew up reading fantasy novels. She later transitioned to urban fantasy and paranormal romance, maybe earlier than it was age appropriate. But don't tell her mother! She now writes paranormal romance, science fiction romance, and reverse harem.

carawylde.com

Guarded by the Golem

Monster Security Agency

First Digital Edition January 2024

GUARDED BY THE GOLEM

CARA WYLDE

MASON

F inding a new job in the private security department after getting fired from Monster Security Agency was impossible. It took me two weeks to realize why. I'd been blacklisted.

It seemed fair seeing how I'd botched my last job, but it wasn't. Because I knew, the client knew, and even my boss knew it hadn't been my fault. I'd warned the stupidly rich idiot not to trust anyone, not even his best friend. I'd protected him with my life, and he went behind my back and almost got himself killed. Fortunately, I got wind of it in time and saved his life, but he still ended up in the hospital with a bullet in his leg, and I still ended up laid off.

I couldn't afford to lose my job. Not now, not ever. Yet it happened, and now I was running all over the city, trying to find work when no one wanted to hire me. If I couldn't be a bodyguard, then what could I be? Could I train others in the field? No one trusted me. When they heard the name Mason Stonewarden, their polite smiles turned into frowns, and they started making up excuses, pretending like they were needed somewhere else.

I was done. My career in private security was over. I'd dedicated years of my life to the MSA, and now they'd thrown me out like yesterday's trash. Monster Security Agency was the best in the business, known for always getting things done, no mistakes. I'd made a mistake and now I was paying for it. I shouldn't have been surprised, but I was, because my boss knew me well, and he knew I was fully dedicated to the job. When I debriefed him about what had happened, he was understanding and sympathetic. But the client was always right, even when the client was dumb. From the hospital, fresh out of surgery, he'd called my boss and asked for my termination.

It wasn't even the first time the MSA had failed me and my family. I should've known better. My brother was the only one who would understand what I was going through, so this morning, instead of heading out to look for a job and find only rejection, I called him and told him I wanted to pay him a visit. He was happy to hear from me.

"Come over for lunch, Mason," he said. "The kids will be home from kindergarten. They've missed you. I'll ask Kara to make your favorite."

My heart ached at my brother's words. He sounded upbeat, like he was having a good day, and I was going to go over there and ruin it for him. At my kitchen table, with only a cup of cold coffee and a stale sandwich to call breakfast, I hung my head and rubbed my bald head. How had it come to this? I was supposed to be the strong one, the one who never gave up, because giving up meant not being able to support my loved ones. My brother, Goliath, and his human wife, Kara, with their two hybrid children, Xavier and Nira, were the most important people in my life. They depended on me, and today, over lunch, I was going to tell them I'd failed them.

I spent the rest of the morning straightening up my apartment and rehearsing in my head how I was going to break it to them that I'd lost my job and couldn't help them with money anymore. I lived in an old building that had been transformed to host monsters of the more humanoid kind, and the rent was high because it was near the city center. If I didn't find work soon, I'd have to look for a new place, probably around where my brother lived. He and his family lived in a neighborhood built by our kind – golems – and they owned their house. I was sure I could find something close to them, but living so far from the city, where I got to mingle with humans and other species, meant it would be even harder to find work that paid well. As golems, we only joined our tight communities when we were ready to settle down.

Not that I wasn't ready to settle down, but with whom? And now that I didn't have a job, it would be even harder to find a wife.

I put on a fresh set of clothes – a buttoned up shirt that wasn't too wrinkled, and a pair of jeans – and got into my truck, knowing it would take me an hour to drive to my brother's place. If I was lucky and traffic was light. I wasn't, and I got stuck on the highway for fifteen minutes, trying to distract myself from my dark thoughts with heavy metal music. Meanwhile, above everyone's heads, creatures with wings had no trouble getting to where they needed to be. Only monsters who couldn't fly drove, and not that I was unhappy with my genetics, but a pair of wings would've served me well in life. I realized it was silly to think like this. My body was heavy, entirely made of stone. There was no way I would've been able to lift myself a foot off the ground.

Being made of stone, essentially indestructible, had its advantages and disadvantages. I was a warrior, born to use my physical strength in the service of others. However, when people looked at me, all they saw was a massive beast who needed to be told what or who to crush. They didn't see what was underneath my rough exterior, couldn't fathom that I, too, had a heart. In time, I came to accept that no one was interested in hearing me express my emotions, so I buried them deep and focused on what was in front of me.

Maybe that was why my brother, Goliath, had married Kara, a human, even if both families had been against their union. She could see him for who he was, even when he looked at himself in the mirror and only saw a block of stone. Today, she was going to see through me, too. It was her gift. She was going to look into my eyes and see what was in my soul, and I was afraid that it would cause me to break down in front of them.

The cars in front started moving. I turned my engine on, and for a second, considered turning back. I wanted to see my brother and his wife, and I missed my niece and nephew. But it was going to be a difficult conversation, made even more uncomfortable by Kara's very much human ability to see through my tough façade.

She was good for Goliath, especially after the accident, when he'd needed so much grace and understanding. I wondered if someone like her would be good for me, too.

Relationships between golems and humans were an oddity. It was better to not get my hopes up. More likely than not, I would one day find someone like me, a female who was tough and made of stone, and together, we would pretend we were unbreakable and had no feelings.

I turned the music up and only turned it back down when I drove into my brother's neighborhood. All the houses here were large, with expansive backyards. Golems needed a lot of space. I pulled into the driveway, parked behind my brother's truck, and as I got out, Xavier and Nira burst out of the house and slammed right into me. I lifted both of them easily, and they screamed as they clung to my thick arms.

"Uncle Mason, we missed you!"

"I missed you too, my favorite rascals."

Their hybrid nature meant they weren't entirely made of stone. Unlike their father and me, they had hair on their little heads. Nira had her mother's blonde hair, and it nearly reached her waist.

Kara appeared in the doorway. She shook her head and came over to give me a kiss on the cheek and retrieve her overenthusiastic toddlers. Behind her, my brother rolled in his wheelchair. His face lit up when he saw me, and I rushed to him so he wouldn't have to cross the driveway.

"Long time," he said. "I always tell you that you should visit more often. You look good!"

"You too, brother."

I was lying. The truth was that since the accident – which hadn't been an accident at all – he'd become smaller, narrower, thinner. His right leg was weaker than ever, and his left leg was only a stump. He'd lost it a year ago, and we hadn't yet managed to raise the money for a good prosthetic that would actually help him be useful again, not hinder him more.

So, after all, golems weren't completely indestructible. With the right weapon, we could get chopped off, too.

We gathered in the large dining room, and Kara enlisted the kids to help her set the table for lunch. I sat across from my brother, and for a few minutes, we just stared at each other.

"It's good to see you," he said.

"Yes."

"I know you're busy."

I cleared my throat and looked away. Plates and glasses materialized on the table as Xavier and Nira made round trips between the kitchen and the dining room.

"Since you hate how busy I am," I said, "You'll be glad to know that has changed recently." I was being sarcastic.

"What do you mean?"

"The MSA dumped me."

He inhaled deeply, exhaled, and shook his head. Over my shoulder, he locked eyes with his wife.

"Kids, go wash your hands," Kara said, before sitting down next to me.

It took me five minutes to tell them the whole story. There wasn't much to tell. I left all emotions out and focused on the facts.

"They've done it again," Kara said. In her voice, I heard anger mixed with sadness. "First Goliath, now you."

My brother had worked for Monster Security Agency, too. He hadn't botched his last job, though. On the contrary, he'd done it so well and put himself in so much danger that he'd lost his left leg. The MSA let him go, because what were they supposed to do with him in a wheelchair? They covered his medical bills but didn't do more than that for him and his family.

It was a job that came with high risks, and we all knew that.

It was the only job I knew how to do.

"Let's eat," Kara said when she noticed the kids had stopped just outside of the dining room to listen to us. She gave them a smile and motioned for them to join us. "Come on. There's no reason to be sad. Everything will be fine."

I shook my head as I stared at the food on my plate. I didn't feel worthy of it, but Kara had made it for me especially, so I ate and asked for seconds. Xavier and Nira started telling me about what they were learning in kindergarten, and their lightheartedness shifted the energy at the table. We ended up laughing and having the best time I remembered us having in months.

After lunch, the kids wanted to play outside, and Kara let them. She made herself busy while Goliath and I talked, listening and chiming in when she noticed the conversation was in danger of taking a depressive turn.

"Mason, you don't have to worry about us," she said at some point. "We're doing okay."

"You're burning through your savings," I said.

She shrugged. "Xavier and Nira are old enough now that I can go back to work." Before marrying my brother and becoming a stay-at-home mom, Kara had worked in sales. "And Goliath will find something, too. It's a little harder, but not impossible."

At least he hadn't been blacklisted.

I rubbed a hand over my face, not knowing what to say. I felt so embarrassed that when my phone vibrated in my pocket, I was relieved I could take a break and step outside. I excused myself and went through the back door, into the yard, where the kids were playing. My relief turned into anger when I saw my boss's name on the screen.

"What?" I barked into the phone.

"Mason. I hope I'm not interrupting anything."

"You are."

"I'll keep this brief, then. I know we haven't parted ways on the best of terms, but a job just came in, and you're the only one who can do it."

MAYA

As soon as I opened my eyes, a pain like I'd never felt before exploded between my temples. My vision was blurry. I blinked rapidly, trying to make sense of what was happening to me. I was surrounded by darkness, I was cold, so stiff that I could barely move, and the pain started seeping through all the muscles in my body. I was lying on the floor, with just a thin mattress to protect me from the rough cement. My shoulders were stiff, and when I tried moving my arms, I realized I was restricted. I felt the bite of metal on my wrists, and panic gripped my chest.

I was cuffed.

Gathering all the strength I could muster, I rolled onto my side and pulled at my restraints. It didn't take me long to realize that the chain was bolted to the floor, a few feet from where my head rested on the old, smelly mattress. I groaned, my head spinning, but I had to push through the panic. Now that I was awake, I couldn't just lie here and accept this. Whatever this was.

I knew what it was. I'd been kidnapped.

I sat up even though every bone in my body protested, tucked my legs under me, and looked around the room. I couldn't distinguish much, and it wasn't just because it was dark and there were no windows. There wasn't much to distinguish. The only objects in the room seemed to be the mattress I was lying on – no pillow and no blanket – and a bucket in a corner. It was within reach, so I stretched toward it, the chains that held my hands tied rattling. I grabbed the bucket and stared into it. It was empty.

I frowned. What was the purpose of it? Did I even want to know?

I pushed the bucket away and crawled toward the bolt in the floor, so the chains would be looser and allow me more range of motion. I rubbed my eyes and forehead, but the headache didn't let up. I ran my hands through my long, tangled hair and discovered it was wet and glued to my scalp at the back of my head. When I looked at my fingers, they were caked with red. Blood.

I must've hit my head, and that was why everything was so muddy and confusing. I couldn't string two coherent thoughts together. Okay, I'd been kidnapped, but how? When? I didn't know what day it was, and to my utter horror, I realized that no matter how hard I tried to remember the last thing I'd done, or the last place I'd been, my mind went blank.

I tried harder. There had to be something. A memory...

What had I done the day before? What was the last thing I ate?

Maybe I was going home, and that was when they took me. Who were they? I tried to remake the itinerary in my head and soon realized that I couldn't picture anything. Not my house, and not the place I was presumably coming from.

Gripped by shock, I sat there with my eyes wide, staring at the wall. Since my memory didn't seem to work, what else could I do for myself right now? Using my awareness, I quickly checked my body to see where it hurt and if I'd been... touched in any way. My muscles ached, but aside from that, I was fine. My head hurt the worst. My clothes were intact, albeit dirty.

"What is happening?" I whispered, just to check that my voice was working. "Who would do such a thing? And to me... Why me?"

I racked my brain for a few more minutes, but it refused to cooperate. I was willing to bet the wound at the back of my head was the culprit. I wondered how I got it. Had someone hit me over the head with something heavy? Had I fallen and hurt myself? So many questions, and not a single answer my brain could deliver.

"Hey!" I yelled or tried to. My voice was weak, so I cleared my throat and tried again. "Hey! Let me out! Help! Help!"

I pulled at the chains, rattling them as loudly as I could. Then I started banging my feet on the ground, all the while screaming for help.

I did this until I tired myself out and my voice stopped working. The headache was so bad that I had to crawl back onto the mattress and lie down. I started crying silently, feeling the tears roll down my face.

I didn't understand why this was happening to me. Did I have enemies? I couldn't remember. Was this random? Had I been in the wrong place at the wrong time? The statistics said that most women were kidnapped by people they knew. It rarely happened that they were kidnapped by strangers. I tried to think really hard about the people in my life, but my mind drew a blank again, and the panic was back, gripping my chest. There was something really wrong with me if I couldn't remember anything.

I heard footsteps beyond the door, and I stilled. They came closer and closer, and then I heard a key in the lock. My heart started galloping in my chest. I sat up again, pulling my knees in and trying to make myself small. The door opened, and there was light on the other side. A shadow appeared in the doorway, and I could tell immediately that it was a man.

"You're awake," he said in a flat tone.

He stepped into the room and closed the door behind him. In his hands, he carried a box. He reached for a string that I now noticed was dangling from the ceiling, pulled it, and a light bulb came to life. It illuminated his face, and I saw he was young, maybe in his late thirties, with black hair and dark eyes that looked dull behind thick-framed glasses. He didn't look like a kidnapper at all. He didn't look like a bad guy. More like a regular guy who seemed mildly bored with everything around him.

"Who are you?" I asked. "Why are you doing this?"

He walked over to me and placed the box on the floor.

"How are you feeling, Maya?"

My eyes widened at the sound of my name. I hadn't thought to check if I remembered my name. I did so now, and it came to me easily – Maya Lucas.

Okay. Maya Lucas. What did Maya Lucas do? Where did she work? Where did she live?

Blank. Blank. Blank.

I felt like crying, but I didn't want to cry in front of him.

"I think I hit my head," I said, testing the waters.

He nodded. "You put on a fight. I hadn't expected you to. Look at you, you're tiny. What were you thinking, kicking and screaming like that? And now you have a concussion. I hope you're proud of yourself."

I couldn't believe his words! So, he was the one who'd kidnapped me. Looking at him, it was true that he was taller, bigger, and stronger than me. I guess I'd never thought a guy with glasses would be capable of something so nefarious.

"Is that why I can't remember anything?"

He cocked an eyebrow. "What do you remember?"

"My name. That's all. And only because you called me Maya, and then it came to me... Maya Lucas."

"That's right. You're Maya Lucas. Before you say I got the wrong person, let me assure you I did not. You're the right person, Maya. Exactly what I need." He crouched down and opened the box. "But I'll need to confirm it by running some tests."

"What?" Inside the box, I saw various types of syringes and glass tubes. There was gauze too, disinfectant, and a few bottles of pills. "What tests? Are you a doctor?"

"Something like that. Relax, I'll just draw a little blood."

"What for?"

"Your arm, Maya."

I thought of fighting him again. But with my wrists cuffed, and in the poor physical state I was in, I didn't think I stood a chance. I extended my right arm toward him, and he proceeded to take a rather generous sample of my blood.

"Please tell me what this is for," I begged. "What are you going to do to me?"

"So many questions," he sighed. "I'll run some tests to make sure that you are, indeed, the person I need. This is a delicate situation, Maya. Your blood must be perfect. If you pass the tests, I'll keep you, and don't worry, I'll take care of you well enough."

"And if I don't pass?"

He shrugged. "Still don't remember anything?"

I furrowed my brows and tried again. Where did Maya Lucas work? Nope. Nothing.

He filled the last tube with blood, then pressed a compress to the puncture in my arm.

"Death will be easier if your memory is gone." He said it so calmly, as if he were talking about the weather. "If it makes you feel any better, I didn't intend to give you a concussion. You made it harder than it had to be. Also, none of this is personal."

"It doesn't make me feel better," I murmured. I was stunned. I was mildly aware I should have been reacting differently, but I was too taken aback by his bored attitude. "So, if I pass the tests, you'll keep me here. Until when?"

"Until you're not useful to me anymore."

He arranged his syringes and tubes in the box, closed it, and stood up.

"Please... I... I didn't do anything to deserve this," I said.

"How do you know, Maya? You just said you remember nothing."

Was he messing with me? Sure, I had no memory of who I was and what my life was like, but I felt deep down that I was a normal person. And normal people didn't do things that warranted such treatment.

"You can't do this," I said.

He pushed his glasses up the bridge of his nose and turned to leave.

"I'll bring you food and water in a bit, then I'll go work on your blood samples."

"You're talking as if..." My voice cracked. "As if this is just another day... As if this is routine."

He opened the door and stepped out. Before closing and locking it, he threw me one last dull glance.

"It is."

MASON

My former boss invited me into his office, then asked his secretary to close the blinds and the door. Monster Security Agency had branches all over the world. This branch was under the management of Taros Mammon, who was a horned devil with flaming eyes and a forked tongue. He sat in his chair, which was made of pure titanium, the only metal that didn't melt when he happened to let his rage reign free. I sat across from him. Without a word, he pushed a contract toward me.

"Is this standard?" I asked.

"Some of it is."

I let out a sigh and read it thoroughly. The MSA provided standard contracts, but there were clients who had specific requirements they wanted added in. Sometimes they were negotiable, most times they weren't. The moment my eyes fell on the clauses that had been added, I knew this job was on the shady side. I looked up at Taros. He knew what my principles were. There were beasts who worked for the MSA and didn't care what the job was. I cared, and I'd always made it a point to avoid jobs that clashed with my values.

"Beggars can't be choosers, Mason," he said.

"Do you think I came here to beg?"

"You came because you need work. This is work."

"You know it wasn't right to fire me," I said.

"The last job you did was a mess, and I don't care whose fault it was."

Fair enough. I could argue and get kicked out of his office, or I could swallow my pride and see this as a second chance.

"Why me?" I asked. "Why did you say on the phone that I'm the only one who can do it?"

He smirked, and I knew him well enough to know what he was going to say was a lie, or at the very least, not the whole truth.

"It's long term. And it's tedious. Only someone as rock-solid and unmoving as you can do it. No pun intended."

"I can see it's long term."

"Yes. If the client likes you, and you do a good job, he will keep you busy for years."

"I gather you don't want your good agents to be stuck in a dead-end job like this."

He shrugged. "It is what it is. But look on the bright side. You'll have a steady income. You'll still work under the MSA, but I won't have to see your face every day and be reminded about how badly you fucked up."

I rolled my eyes. "Fine." I scribbled my name on the contract and pushed it over to him.

The truth was, I had no choice. I didn't know what the job was, just that it sounded unusual. I was going to find out soon enough.

"This is the address." Taros scribbled it on a piece of paper. "For your eyes only. Commit it to memory and burn it. Now get out of my sight." He smirked. "And good luck."

I gave him a nod and a grunt, since his attitude didn't warrant more than that.

The address took me outside of the city. My first thought was that the commute was going to be a pain, but then I remembered the clause in the contract that said it was a live-in position. The client needed me on the job twenty-four-seven. If this worked out, I could give up the apartment and keep the rent money. As I stopped in front of a massive gate, I shook my head at my premature thoughts. It was never a good idea to get ahead of myself.

I found myself in front of a gated estate, and I had to push a button and wait for a crackling voice on the other end to interrogate me before letting me in. Apparently, my new client took his security very seriously. He was waiting for me in front of his impressive mansion. As I got out of my truck, he didn't make any move toward me. He waited for me to walk over to him and didn't look like he would shake my hand if I offered.

Also, he was human.

"Mason Stonewarden," he said in a rather blasé voice.

"Yes, that's me. I'm your new bodyguard."

"I'm Dr. Vincent Lockwood. Please follow me."

This guy wasn't friendly at all. He was tall and lean – tall for his kind, at least – with dark hair that was neatly combed away from his large forehead. He wore glasses that he often pushed up the bridge of his nose,

GUARDED BY THE GOLEM   25

and a white lab coat over his dark, perfectly ironed clothes. He was all business.

I wondered what kind of doctor he was. My job, however, wasn't to ask questions, but to follow orders. In my line of work, some clients I had to know inside out to be able to protect, and other clients I didn't have to know at all. Dr. Vincent Lockwood fell into the second category.

On the inside, the mansion was even more impressive than on the outside. Immediately, I could tell that it belonged to a family that came from money, generation after generation. It was decorated in a gaudy way that somehow didn't lack taste completely. We crossed the entry hall, then Dr. Lockwood led me through a set of corridors until we reached the back of the house. He didn't invite me into any of the rooms on the first floor, and frankly, I was a little disappointed. I would've loved to see what the living room looked like, and I was sure there was a library, too, and maybe a game room. These types of mansions always had it all.

Next, he led me down a set of stairs, and the more we descended beneath the house, the more uneasy I felt. Finally, we reached a chamber that was dark and humid, entirely made of stone and cement. This was the basement. Instead of wine racks filled with old, fancy bottles, there was a bed in a corner, a desk, and a chair. There were two doors, one on the left, one on the right. The one on the left was open, and I glimpsed a rudimentary bathroom. The one on the right was closed.

"This is you," Dr. Lockwood said.

I stared at him like he was speaking an alien language.

"This is your post. You have a mini fridge over there." Right, I hadn't noticed the fridge. It was that mini. "I will make sure you have everything you need, of course. I will have food delivered, any drinks of choice, no alcohol."

"Alcohol doesn't have an effect on me."

"That's good to know. My housekeeper will clean and change the sheets once a week. You have a bathroom that's perfectly functional."

"And all I have to do is…"

"Guard that door."

He pointed at the door on the right.

When he said, "guard that door", what he meant was "guard what's behind the door". What was behind the door? Riches? Stacks of money? Gold bars? Precious gems? No, that was silly. No one kept that sort of stuff in their basement.

"And this is long term," I said, hoping I could gauge more information.

"Yes. I wasn't sure until this morning. I ran some tests, got the results I was looking for, and now I need you to guard that door with your life. Can you do that?"

"And if you ran those tests and didn't get the results you were looking for?"

He thought for a second, then said, "This would've been a cleaning job and much shorter than a guarding job."

Had I had any hairs on my body, they would've bristled.

"I don't do cleaning jobs."

"That's irrelevant now, isn't it? I'll ask again. Can you do the job?"

"Yes. Yes, I can."

"Good. Now, go home, get your things in order, and pack what you need. You start tomorrow."

He started up the stairs, but I didn't follow him immediately. I stared at the closed door for a long minute, knowing it was locked and knowing that whatever was behind it was none of my business. I knew this job was shady, and I took it anyway. No going back now.

Monster Security Agency didn't discriminate. As long as the client paid, no one cared if what he asked for was illegal or not. Most jobs were bodyguard jobs, though, and that was what I was good at. I could guard a door. Of course I could.

But if Dr. Lockwood hadn't gotten the results he wanted, this would've been a cleaning job. Whatever was behind that door wasn't an object. It was a living, breathing creature. Of what kind, I didn't know, and my client didn't seem interested in offering me that information.

It didn't matter. I was here to do what I was told, and from the looks of it, this was going to be an easy job, and paid quite handsomely, too.

Moral compass or no moral compass, I wasn't in a position to refuse it.

MAYA

I could hear voices on the other side of the door. One was my captor's, the other one was unknown to me. All I wanted was to scream, make noise, ask for help, draw the other person's attention, but I couldn't. My captor had made sure of it.

Before he went to retrieve his visitor, he brought a chair into my room, bolted it to the floor, right before my eyes, so I saw I couldn't use it as a weapon, then forced me into it, tied me up, and duct-taped my mouth.

I couldn't move an inch. I could groan, but that wasn't enough. I tried to bang my feet on the floor, but the bastard had tied me up so well that it was impossible to do anything that made a loud noise. I wasn't strong enough to topple the chair with me in it, and he'd made sure to bolt it perfectly.

He was very strategic, my captor. Calculated. He only made a move when he knew he had all the pieces in place. This morning, when he'd brought me breakfast and exactly one glass of water, he'd told me my blood had passed his tests. He was going to keep me.

Oh, and the bucket? I found out quickly what it was for, when I had to pee and realized there was no bathroom. My captor had emptied and cleaned it this morning without a word.

At this point, I just wanted to know why he was going through so much trouble to keep me here. If I knew, maybe I could come up with some sort of plan to convince him to let me go. I had to convince him, because it didn't look like he was ever going to loosen up the security measures he had in place to give me a chance to escape. I'd been here for two days. Maybe three? I wasn't sure... The point was I'd been here for a while, and I'd been chained all this time. I hadn't even made it to the door once, let alone had the chance to try it or slam into it to see if I could make it budge.

The voices continued for a while. They were subdued, and I couldn't understand what they were saying. I had no idea who my captor had brought. It was a male voice, and deep down, even though I had some hope left that someone would come rescue me, I knew I couldn't trust a man. It was entirely possible that they were in cahoots. Not that I had been hard to kidnap, but it did seem like an operation for at least two people. My captor probably worked with others. If I ever saw anyone else enter this room, I had to remind myself I couldn't trust them.

I heard their footsteps as they paced the floor, and then I heard them fading. For a while, it was quiet. Then I heard footsteps again, and it seemed like my captor was alone. I knew what he sounded like – light on his feet. The other man had sounded heavy and much bigger, which was not a detail that made me feel better about my prospects.

The key turned in the lock, and my captor walked in with a tray of food.

"I'm sorry, Maya, but you understand. There will be some instances when I will have to make sure you don't cause a scene."

I looked up at him, unable to do anything. I just stared into his eyes, hoping he would show some kind of emotion, but he remained cold and heartless. I couldn't understand how he could do this to me. He wasn't a monster. At least not in the sense that he was of a different species than me. He was human, and he was doing this to another human. To a woman who couldn't protect herself. He was sick beyond anything I could've imagined possible.

I waited for him to untie me. He placed the food tray on the ground, then slowly undid the restraints around my ankles.

"Don't try anything stupid," he said. "You can't overpower me. Last time, you gave yourself a concussion."

Right. My head still throbbed, and I was in constant pain. He'd patched up my wound and given me painkillers, but not too many, saying something about how he didn't want the pills to spoil my blood. I had no clue why my blood was so important to him. He was almost obsessed with it.

He untied my hands, but immediately cuffed them to the chain that was bolted to the floor. Finally, he removed the duct tape. I took a deep breath and shot him a stare that was filled with hatred. He passed me the glass of water he'd brought, and I accepted it with shaking hands. I was thirsty all the time. He only allowed me three glasses a day, with the three meals he delivered himself.

"Doesn't dehydration affect the quality of my blood?" I asked.

"I'll bring you a few bottles of water. Don't abuse my generosity, though."

I huffed. "Your generosity?"

"You should be grateful, Maya. I'm taking good care of you."

I looked around me. The bucket in a corner, the chair that was bolted to the floor, the filthy mattress I was sitting on. Was he delusional? Maybe he needed a new prescription for his eyeglasses.

He sat on the floor, legs crossed, and placed the tray on my lap. He didn't take his eyes off me. I dug in, knowing he wasn't going to leave until I finished eating, so he could take the tray. Just in case I thought of using it, or the plastic plates and utensils, to make some sort of rudimentary weapon.

"Do you want to know who that was?" he asked.

I didn't say anything.

"I hired a bodyguard," he continued. "Just for you. I told you I care about you a lot, Maya. You're important to me. In fact, right now, you're the most important thing I own."

At his words, the tiny hairs on my arms stood on end. Anger boiled in my chest, and I pushed it down. He didn't own me. Whatever he said, it wasn't true, and I had to remind myself of that. He was impossible to argue with, so I wasn't going to try.

"This bodyguard is expensive, but I think it will be worth it in the long run. He starts tomorrow. So, enjoy a little freedom today. Move around, exercise a little. I'll have to tie you up again in the morning. I'll be in my lab all day, and I don't need you causing a commotion."

"Does this mean…" I wasn't sure what I wanted to say, how to express myself. My head was killing me, and it felt like my brain was glitching. It happened a lot when I tried to think really hard about something or make sense of something my captor said. "Does this mean he doesn't know what he's guarding?"

He grinned. "He will realize soon enough. By that time, however, he will have understood how easy this job is and won't want to jeopardize it. Plus, you're none of his business. I hired him, I'm paying him, so he will follow my orders. He can't do anything for you, Maya. Okay? Get that into your head because I know what you're thinking. You hope that if you get a chance to talk to him and play victim, he will help you. He won't. I'll tie you up, anyway. Just the first few days, until he gets used to his new posting. We'll see how it goes."

I couldn't take another bite. He noticed and frowned.

"Finish your meal," he said. "You won't get anything else until dinner."

"I'm not hungry anymore."

"You will be hungry later."

"Just leave it here, then. What are you so afraid of?"

He squinted at me, unhappy with my attitude, then pushed his glasses up his nose.

"Fine. You can have the plate. No fork, though."

As if I could do anything with a cheap plastic fork.

He got up. Before leaving, he checked my cuffs and the chain.

"Why are you doing this?" I asked, though I knew it was futile.

He was silent, as usual, and I thought he wasn't going to answer me this time, either. Since he'd brought me here, I'd been asking him over and over. I needed to understand. What had I done to deserve this? What was his end goal? I needed some kind of explanation, especially since my memories were still blurry at best and I couldn't come up with any explanations myself.

"If you must know... If it will make you feel better," he started, "I'm doing it for the most important person in my life."

"What? I thought I was..."

"No, you're confused. I said you are the most important thing I own. You're a thing, Maya. An object. And you are here because this is the only way I can help the most important person in my life. So, you're doing a good thing. Probably the only good thing you ever did."

"I don't understand..." I touched my temple with my trembling fingers. "Who is this person?"

"Enough with the questions. I've told you too much already." He turned away. "Eat your food, or it will spoil."

He locked the door behind him, and I was alone again, surrounded by darkness. I pushed the plate away and huddled under the blanket that he'd given me the day before. I'd complained about being cold, and he'd brought me a pillow and a blanket. Soon enough, I'd have to complain about my clothes, which absolutely stank. If I didn't point out these things to him, he didn't notice them. It was as if he had no idea what a human being needed to survive, although he was a human being himself.

Or maybe he wasn't. Maybe the species didn't matter at all. Humans could lack a heart and a soul, too.

MASON

My second day on the job, and did it irk me I didn't know who I was guarding? Yes, it did.

It was confirmed to me that it was a person when I first saw Dr. Lockwood come down to the basement with a tray of food and a bottle of water. He did it three times a day, like clockwork. But this detail alone wasn't enough for me to gauge who he had in there, if they were human or something else, if they were male or female.

I didn't ask questions. I wasn't supposed to. Being clear to me this was nowhere near legal, I knew any questions I asked might get me in trouble and cause me to lose my job. And I needed this job. It paid more than the last few I'd done for Monster Security Agency, and within one or two months, I could have the money my brother needed to get himself a good prosthetic. It would be life-changing for him and his family, so I needed to keep my eyes on the prize.

Whatever happened behind the door I was guarding was none of my business.

However, I couldn't help but notice that twice already, Dr. Lockwood had gone in there carrying a medical kit. He was a scientist, so it wasn't like it didn't make sense, but at the same time, what did that mean? That he was doing experiments on whoever he had in there? I couldn't think about that. I had to shut off my thoughts.

I was the muscle and nothing more. I wasn't supposed to have thoughts.

As for me, I was well taken care of. The bed could've been considered big for a human, but for me, it was regular. The sheets were new and freshly washed, and the mattress was comfortable enough. I had a desk and two chairs, though Dr. Lockwood never sat down for a chat. I'd brought a few books in my bag, along with some clothes, so I had something to keep myself busy. When I wasn't reading, I was scrolling on my tablet. Surprisingly, I had decent Wi-Fi even if I was pretty deep underground.

The bathroom wasn't much, but I didn't need more than a sink, a toilet, and a shower. I had to appreciate the fact that it was built to fit my massive frame. That made me wonder if Dr. Lockwood had known he was going to hire me when he'd prepared this chamber and the bathroom. Maybe he knew he was going to hire a monster, and generally, monsters were big fellows.

I could live like this. If I was paid enough, it was no big deal. It bothered me a little that there were no windows down here, but I could take breaks and walk outside into the sun. I did so three times a day, when my client was inside the room. When he came with food and water, the first thing he did was to tell me I could take a break if I wanted to. He waited for me to leave, and then went inside the room that was such a mystery to me. I didn't know what it looked like and who it was hosting. It didn't sound like an order when he told me I could take a half-hour stroll in the garden, so I didn't think much of it at first. I was grateful I could get out for a bit. But the third time it happened, I started wandering...

It was lunchtime, and as always, Dr. Lockwood showed up with the food and water.

"Take a break, Mason," he said.

I pretended like I was deeply absorbed by the book I was reading. Which meant I ignored him to give him the impression that I hadn't even noticed his presence.

"Mason, I said you can take a break."

"Oh?" I blinked in slight confusion. "Oh, right. I'm fine. I want to finish this chapter." And I immediately returned to the book.

He stood there for a minute, staring at me. I thought he was going to insist, but eventually, he unlocked the door and slipped inside. I couldn't look, or I would've given myself away. I felt a thrill travel up my spine. He'd never unlocked the door in my presence, and I noticed he didn't lock it behind him. I couldn't help but wonder what that meant.

If the one inside was here against their will, then they would try to escape, right? They would make a run for the door. Dr. Lockwood wasn't a big guy. Someone who had enough determination could easily knock him down.

The other possibility was that they weren't here against their will. Then what was I guarding the door for?

I turned slightly in my chair so the door would be in my line of sight when it opened again. I turned the page, just in case Dr. Lockwood had paid attention, but I couldn't read a single word. I fully focused on what was going on behind the door, straining to hear any sounds that might give it away.

And there it was... A cry. Whispers, and then someone sniffling, crying silently. Dr. Lockwood's voice rose, and I could tell he was chastising his victim. The victim who sounded like... a woman.

I slammed the book on the table and sat up straight. He had a woman in there, and she sure didn't sound like it was her choice. Heat spread through my body, angry and red. I forced myself to wait. I could barge in there, but I didn't think it was a good idea. Dr. Lockwood wouldn't like it, and if the woman needed my help, a premature intervention on my part would do her more harm than good. I had to be calculated. Like him.

Though I was nothing like him. He didn't seem to have any feelings. I had a temper.

After half an hour, he reemerged with the tray, the plate on it empty. He looked at me and nodded, seemingly unaware that I was boiling on the inside.

"You should've taken a break, Mason. Now you'll have to wait until dinner."

"I heard something," I said. I did my best to keep my voice steady. "Do you have a woman in there? A woman who's crying?"

His shoulders tensed, but that was the only reaction he showed.

"That's none of your business," he said.

"Is she in there by choice? Because if not, I don't think I can do this job, Dr. Lockwood. If it means hurting someone..."

"Please. You hurt people all the time."

"To protect my clients, yes."

"This job is no different from the others you did," he said.

"If you're holding a woman against her will and you hired me to make sure she doesn't escape, it's different. This is not the kind of job I do."

"Why not?"

"It doesn't sit well with me. It's against my principles."

He laughed. "Principles. You have those." His face turned serious, which took me aback. It was uncanny how he could switch from one expression to another. "All right. What if I told you this woman is dangerous?" He pointed at the door. "What if I told you she hurt someone I care deeply about? Someone I love."

My eyes widened. "I would ask if it's true."

"Why would I lie to you, Mason?"

So many reasons. I didn't know a lot about Dr. Vincent Lockwood, but I could read people well enough to know this one wasn't to be trusted.

"I hired you to do a job," he said. "Not ask questions, not question my methods. It doesn't matter who's in there. All that matters is that you guard this door. No one goes in besides me."

Interesting. He wasn't afraid that the woman might escape. He was afraid someone might... come save her?

"So, is she dangerous?" I asked. "Who did she hurt?"

"My mother," he said.

Well, that shut me up fast. I nodded, and he didn't say another word, just turned on his heel and left, like I'd offended him.

I hung my head and closed my eyes, trying to make sense of what he'd just told me. Aside from him and the housekeeper, I hadn't seen anyone else in the house. Oh, and the gardener. Was his mother alive, or was she dead? Was Dr. Lockwood messing with my head?

I believed he was. The answers he gave me were always clipped and meant to confuse. It was up to me to read between the lines, which was not something I was great at. I was good with physical things. But emotions, mental challenges, intellectual stuff... I was trying to better myself through reading, but I wasn't nearly there. I felt like I needed a course in psychology to understand my client.

I looked at the door. There was a woman in there. In a room with no windows and no light. I'd just seen that Dr. Lockwood turned on a light bulb when he went in and turned it off when he walked out. Had she really done what he was accusing her of? Was she human, like him? Because if she was, I didn't know if I could do this for another day, let alone long term. What plans did he have for her? Obviously, it wasn't all about revenge.

I was going to have to do this my way and get the answers I needed. I had to be smart.

MAYA

I didn't know how long it had been, but it had become unbearable. During the day, my captor left me gagged and tied to the chair. He released me when he came in to feed me, and then he only removed the gag after I assured him with nods and gestures that I wouldn't scream. I had to play nice, otherwise he would stop feeding me. I was certain he was capable of it. At night, he allowed me on the mattress, but he cuffed my hands in such a way that I couldn't remove the duct tape from my mouth. I was so uncomfortable all the time that I was shocked my body could still function somewhat normally.

Because of the bodyguard that he'd posted at the door, now I had to use the bucket when my captor was in the room with me. It was so mortifying that I could only do it if I really had to go, and I mentally checked out first. He had the decency to keep his back turned, at least.

When I was alone, I told myself over and over that at least I was alive, and at least he hadn't touched me or tortured me. All he did was draw blood once in a while. It was my mantra – "I'm alive, I'm alive, I'm alive. That's all that matters." I was slowly losing it, though. I had nightmares and woke up drenched in sweat, wishing I was dead. Twice I'd had half the mind to ask him to kill me. Just kill me and be done with it. I only stopped myself from saying it out loud because I knew he needed me, so he wouldn't do it. I'd just be degrading myself even more asking for it.

I kept trying to remember details about my life. My wound had stopped throbbing, and the headaches were nearly gone. All things considered, my body was doing one hell of a job healing. A few things started coming back to me...

I was Maya Lucas, and I was a kindergarten teacher. Yes, that was right. The memory came to me in a flash of colors – children laughing and playing, singing and asking me questions about all the things under the sun. I knew it was true because when I remembered the children's faces, I felt my heart fill with love and joy. Names came to me, too. Sara, and Hannah, and Norbert. My favorite students. They say a teacher shouldn't have favorites, but of course I did. All the other teachers did, too. Christina. That was one of my colleagues. We sometimes went out for coffee. I considered her my friend.

Did they miss me? Only if I was a good teacher. I believed I was. I felt it deep in my heart. I tried to unearth more memories, but my mind drew a blank again. It didn't want to cooperate more than it was ready to cooperate. I wondered if it was because of the concussion, or if my captor was doing something to me, giving me drugs I wasn't aware of. The food and water could've contained anything.

For hours, I entertained myself with the few memories of my young students playing and chasing each other, pulling at my sleeve or my pants when they wanted something and were too enthusiastic to wait. These images kept me sane. The hours passed, and I replayed the scenes in my head over and over, while repeating to myself in the background, "I am alive, I am alive."

Then I heard the key in the lock, and my heart skipped a beat. Every time he came to see me, even if he brought food and water, he also brought me back to this room and reminded me I wasn't a free woman anymore. He had his medical kit with him.

"I need a bit more blood, Maya. I hope that's okay."

I didn't have the strength to look at him and confront him with my usual death glare. He untied me, made me nod a promise that I wouldn't scream, then removed the duct tape. I smacked my lips and accepted the bottle of water he offered.

"How about I don't tie you back up this time? Promise you'll be a good, silent girl, and I won't even cuff you. You can roam around the room for the first time. What do you think?"

"I'd like that," I whispered.

He helped me sit on the mattress, filled a tube with my blood, and even put cream on the wounds around my wrists. The metal cuffs had bitten into my skin so many times that it was raw and bruised.

"Eat."

It felt like such a miracle to have my hands completely free for once. I ate quickly because I knew he didn't like spending more than half an hour with me at a time. I looked peaceful on the outside, maybe even grateful, but my mind was going a hundred miles an hour. Now that I was free to roam, I could finally reach the door. I knew it was unlocked. He never locked it when he was in here, but that was because he always kept me cuffed. Was this an oversight on his part?

I also knew something else. Every time he came down to the basement, he told the bodyguard to take a break. He once told him loud enough that I could hear him.

This was my chance. It could've been my only chance. The door was unlocked, I was fed, and the guard was on his break. If I took my captor by surprise, I could push him to the ground before he knew what was happening, rush to the door, and then up the stairs – because, of course, there would be stairs. Could I do it? Was I strong enough? Was I fast enough?

I had to try.

I couldn't think, I just had to do it. I needed a distraction, something that would throw him off, even for a moment. I reached for the bottle of water. It was half full, with the cap off since I'd just drunk from it. Making my hand shake visibly, I knocked it over, causing it to roll away from the mattress, water spilling everywhere.

"Oh, I'm so sorry. I didn't mean to... I feel so weak..."

He shook his head and reached for the bottle. That was my cue. I jumped to my feet, pushed him away with one hand, and sprinted to the door. For a second, I thought I was going to make it. My knees felt like jelly, and my feet tingled from being tied up around my ankles for so many hours, but I pushed on. I gave it my all.

He caught me from behind, his hand gripping my shirt. I heard the fabric rip, and I slammed into the door. I scrambled for the door handle, but he wrapped one arm around my waist and pulled me away.

"Help!" I started screaming, even though I knew no one could hear me. "No! Let go! Let go of me, please! I can't take this anymore! Help! Help!"

All I managed was to bang on the door a few times. The door handle was out of my reach, and then he was dragging me back into the depths of the room, slamming me into the chair that I hated so much. I fought him with all my might, which meant very little, since I was so weak that I didn't even comprehend how my body wasn't falling apart. He overpowered me easily and secured my hands first, then my feet. I slumped in the chair as he taped my mouth.

"I don't appreciate this at all, Maya. You promised you would behave, and then you did the opposite. I don't enjoy doing this to you, you know. I would've let you move freely around the room, sleep comfortably with your hands uncuffed. Look what you're making me do. I wanted to be nice to you, show you kindness, and you had to disappoint me."

I started crying silently. My vision was blurry, my head hurt, and I was exhausted. I just wanted him to go and leave me with my shame.

I'd failed. There was no escaping this nightmare. And now that I'd proved to him I couldn't be trusted, I was worse off.

MASON

How could I play this? I only had minutes to decide.

The woman Lockwood kept in the room didn't want to be here. She was in pain, close to her limit. Could I trust him that he was doing this because she deserved it? Because she'd hurt his mother somehow, and now he was exacting revenge? He was odd for a human. Generally, humans were emotional compared to monsters. They let themselves be led by their feelings. But Lockwood had shown no feelings since I'd met him. He was hard to read.

I needed to see the captive with my own eyes. If I couldn't read him, then maybe I could read her. The way she screamed, begged, and banged on the door made me feel rage deep inside my belly. She was helpless, and he was torturing her. I had to do something, but I had to be smart about it. I had no idea what was going on here.

After a few more minutes, Lockwood emerged with the empty food tray and his medical kit. The plan I'd made in my head was rudimentary, and its success depended on my acting fast, taking him by surprise.

I crossed the room in two long strides and pinned him against the door as soon as he'd locked it. He dropped everything and used his hands to push me away.

"What are you doing?" He didn't sound frightened. More like... demanding. "Stand down, guard. What's gotten into you?"

I could crush him with my little finger. I wasn't going to do it just yet.

"Who do you have in there?" I asked.

He was trapped between the door and my chest. I held my hands by my sides, if only to stop myself from wringing his neck.

"Someone who's paying for her sins," he said.

As vague as ever.

"Stand down," he said in a lower tone now. "Or don't, if you want to lose your job."

I backed away, and he took a deep, calming breath, exhaled as if he needed a moment to compose himself and forgive me for my transgression, then straightened his clothes and pushed his glasses up his nose.

"Do you swear she did something to your mother and you're only making her pay for it?" I asked.

"I don't have to swear it, and I don't have to tell you anything. I didn't expect you to be so difficult. I'll have to call your boss and have a talk with him about what you just did."

He picked up the medical kit, then kicked the tray in my direction. The plastic plates and utensils left bits of food on the cement floor.

"Clean this up, since it's your mess."

With that, he left, his footsteps as measured and lightweight as ever. To be fair, the guy mystified me. And maybe even scared me a little. His confidence was off the charts. Did he really think his money could buy me, and that he had power over me just because he'd signed a contract with Monster Security Agency? Legally, sure, he did. Legally and professionally, I was required to do what he said with no questions asked. But I wasn't like that. I might've not been a saint or a hero, but I had my morals.

I waited a beat, then pulled out the key from my pocket. I could be stealthy when I wanted to. Attacking Lockwood had merely been a distraction, so I could get my hands on the key. I didn't know how long it would take him to realize it was missing, so I pushed it into the lock and turned it.

I cracked the door quietly, wary of what I would find inside. A sliver of light penetrated the darkness, guiding my gaze from the toes of my boots, over the cement floor, to a set of tiny feet tied to a chair. My gaze moved upward – slender legs, thin arms, a long neck, bright blue eyes swimming in tears. She was tied up so tightly that she couldn't move an inch. Her mouth was covered with duct tape.

I cursed under my breath, not believing that Lockwood was capable of something like this. No, in fact, I did believe it. He was a psychopath. I stepped inside, closed the door, and switched on the only light bulb. She winced, her eyelids fluttering in discomfort.

She was tiny, with long brown hair and the biggest, most beautiful eyes I had ever seen. She looked at me with hope and despair, not knowing what to expect. I approached her carefully, holding my hands up.

"Hey there. I'm Mason. The bodyguard. I mean you no harm. Here's what I'm going to do. I will untie you, so we can talk. I don't know what's happening here, just that I was hired to guard the door. I want to hear your story, okay?"

She nodded.

"It's important that you don't scream. I stole the key from Dr. Lockwood, and I don't know how long it will take him to figure it out. We don't have much time, so let's use every second of it wisely."

She nodded again. Now that we were in agreement, I started moving a bit quicker. I undid the ropes around her legs and arms, and peeled off the duct tape. I was ready to cover her mouth in case she screamed, but she surprised me by being calm and cooperative.

"What's your name?" I asked.

"Maya. Maya Lucas."

I helped her out of the chair and onto the mattress that was on the floor, against the back wall. She looked terrible. Her gaze traveled quickly to a chain that ended with two handcuffs, and I shuddered when I realized it was bolted to the floor. All this time, she'd been tied up or chained? How long had she been here?

"Please help me," she whispered. "Please stop him."

I kneeled before her, blocking the way to the door. I was so big compared to her that even from this position, I was several heads taller than her. She had to crane her neck to look at me. I didn't know who I was dealing with, so I was taking things slowly, not jumping to conclusions, but it seemed preposterous to think that Maya had hurt anyone and deserved this. Still, I had to hear it from her.

"What did you do to Lockwood's mother?"

"Who's Lockwood?" she asked.

I frowned. "The one who put you in here."

"That's his name? I had no idea."

"Dr. Vincent Lockwood," I said, knowing full well that if this went south, and he found out she knew his name, he might decide to get rid of her. I didn't know how things were going to unfold from here on out, but deep down, I was already certain I wasn't going to let him touch her again. "His mother," I continued, "Is she dead? Still alive?"

"What? I don't know what you're talking about. How would I know? I didn't even know his name.

Is this what he told you? That I did something to his mother?"

"Yes. Looking at you, though... I think he's lying. I know he's lying."

I expected her to jump on that and confirm that he was a lying psycho bastard, but instead, Maya averted her gaze and hug her knees to her chest.

"Maya? What's wrong?"

She looked so small and helpless, so exhausted and beaten up that I felt a powerful urge to wrap her in my arms and cradle her while I promised her the head of Vincent Lockwood on a silver platter.

"My name is all I can remember," she said. "My name and my job. I'm a kindergarten teacher." She reached a hand behind her head. "When he kidnapped me, I fought him, apparently. My memory is gone. It's because I hit my head and got a concussion. I didn't think a concussion could be so bad. I get flashes sometimes, images that pop into my head, but I can't always make sense of them. I feel like my memories are just out of reach. When I try to push and remember, I get these terrible headaches."

I clenched my jaw and squeezed my hands into fists, imagining Lockwood's brain matter slip through my fingers as I crushed his skull.

Maya looked up at me again. "What I'm trying to say is… Mason, right? That's your name."

"Mason Stonewarden."

She smiled. "That's a unique name. I like it. Mine is so boring. Anyway, what I want to say is… You're here to get my side of the story, but I don't know what it is. I know he kidnapped me, and he's been keeping me here for a few days. He feeds me but doesn't care about me. He draws my blood once in a while and does something with it in his lab. That's all I know, and most of it, he's told me himself. So, I don't know if I did anything to his mother… I just don't. If I repeat his name to myself… Vincent Lockwood, Vincent Lockwood… my mind draws a blank. I can't remember if I know him or not. I don't think I do, but my thoughts are so jumbled."

She hung her head and pressed her hands to her eyes. Slowly, she started rocking back and forth.

"You couldn't have," I said. "Look at you! A kindergarten teacher?"

"I don't know… I don't know…"

"Maya." My hands shot out before I could stop them. They landed on her arms, and she startled when she felt my touch. "Maya, listen to me. Look deep inside, reach deep down, and tell me what you feel the truth is."

"Mason, I..."

"Just do it. Go with your gut, not with your confused thoughts. That's all because of the concussion and the trauma that piece of trash has put you through."

She looked up at me, and I noticed she wasn't shaking anymore. She didn't push me away, though I was probably squeezing her quite hard. I let heat spread through my body, down into my hands and fingers, and let that heat – the heat of my body – warm her. It was a soothing kind of heat, not the kind that was red and filled with rage, like I'd felt earlier for Lockwood.

Few people could draw this heat out of me. It was the heat of my heart, not the heat of my belly.

"I feel like," she started hesitantly, "I feel like... I wouldn't hurt anyone. I work with children. I remember some of my students. Their names and their faces... I feel like someone who loves children could never do what Lockwood is accusing me of. What do you think?"

"I think you should trust your intuition because I do. You didn't do anything, Maya. He's lying."

"Why, though?"

"I don't know."

I got up to my feet and extended a hand to her. She stared at it but didn't take it.

"I'm getting you out of here," I said. "Come on."

She thought for a moment, then shook her head.

"Maya, come on. You have nothing to be afraid of. I will take care of you. I will crush him and take you far away from here."

"No," she said.

I couldn't believe my ears. "What?"

"No, Mason. Not yet. I want to know."

"Know what?"

"Why he's doing this to me. Why he hired you to guard the door when he knows full well he's already made it impossible for me to escape. Now that I have you on my side and I know I can trust you, I can take this... I can take his torture for a little while longer."

"Maya, don't do this. Let's just get out of here."

"I need to know, or what's happened to me means nothing at all. I've suffered so much... I need it to mean something. Please."

I let out a deep sigh. I turned away and paced the room, rubbing my bald head with my hands, feeling so frustrated that I could crush my own skull.

"Mason, please," she whispered.

"If this is what you want..."

"It is."

I nodded. "All right. But I won't let him touch you again. Do you hear me, Maya? He touches you, he loses both hands."

MAYA

Mason was a golem. When I saw him, I knew it immediately, which was great news. It meant my memories weren't lost forever. Little by little, they would come back to me. I'd seen golems before, around the city, though I'd never interacted with them. And that was how another piece of information returned to me – I lived in a neighborhood where only humans lived. And my job... my job was in the same neighborhood! I didn't have to go to the city center too often, which meant I rarely saw and talked to monsters.

When he'd touched me, I'd felt this soothing heat seep into my bones. He made me feel safe. More than that, he made me feel brave. Had it not been for him, for his imposing presence, I wouldn't have had the courage to stay when I could've escaped. As I asked him to help me find out why Lockwood was doing this to me, I couldn't believe it myself. I'd never been or felt so brave in my life. I was sure it was because of Mason.

I wondered what he was going to do. He hadn't tied me back up, and I was free to walk around the room and stretch properly for the first time in days. Oh, how I wished I could wash myself! How I wished I could brush my teeth, wash my hair, change my clothes! Mason was truly a good person if he saw me in the state I was in and didn't judge me.

What about me? Was I a good person?

My captor had told him I'd done something to his mother. Mason didn't believe it, and I didn't believe it either, but seeing how I couldn't remember a damn thing, I couldn't be sure. And I wanted to be sure, because the accusation was terrible, and if I'd done something wrong and hurt someone, I wanted to know about it, understand the extent of the harm I'd caused.

Was I being gaslit? That could be a possibility, too. Lockwood was strange. He had this uncanny aura about him, where I couldn't tell if he felt emotions or not. He saw himself as being kind and generous just because he fed me three times a day, and when he tied me up and gagged me, he seemed convinced that I was forcing him to do it with my bad behavior. He'd told me the concussion was my fault because I'd fought him.

That did sound like gaslighting.

Still, I couldn't help but wonder about his mother. Like Mason, I wanted to know if she was alive. And well. I hoped she was well. No matter who her son was and what he did, no mother deserved to suffer.

With my arms above my head, I rose on my tiptoes and stretched as high as I could. My back popped in a few places, and I focused on my breath. As tired as I was, and as much as I wanted to just lie down and stare at the ceiling, I knew that my body needed to move. I considered doing some push-ups, working out a bit. Like I'd seen people do in movies when they were trapped somewhere with no way to escape.

Mason Stonewarden.

I'd meant it when I told him I liked his name. Monsters had such interesting names. Humans, not so much.

He didn't think I deserved this. Even if I had done something bad that I couldn't remember, I felt like Mason would still not think I deserved to be treated this way, and that made me feel confident and secure.

Not knowing who I was, what I'd done or didn't do, how I lived my life... all these gaps in my memory made me feel like I could be anyone, that I could be any kind of person, a bad one included.

Was Mason right to trust me? I hoped he was. He'd just met me, though, and he didn't know anything about me. And I couldn't tell him, either.

Okay, now I was having doubts again. My pacing became frantic, and I felt like the room wasn't big enough. It was like a cage, and I couldn't breathe. I had to stop thinking about things that put me in a dark mood.

Mason was good. It was good that he'd found me, that he'd untied me and wanted to help me. I would not doubt any of that, no matter how confused I was.

The wait was killing me. Beyond the door, everything seemed to be silent. After Mason had left, I'd heard him pace for a while, but then he'd stopped, leaving me to wonder what he was doing and what he was thinking about. I didn't want to talk to him through the door in case Lockwood came down and heard us.

Dr. Vincent Lockwood. The name still didn't ring a bell. And what was he doing with my blood? Lab tests, for sure, but of what sort? I needed to know. Because it was my blood and my life. It was easy to escape now that a golem – a man who was massive and literally made of stone – was on my side, but I refused to leave this place until I got some answers.

Besides, if I escaped now, who was to say it would be safe for me to go back home and get on with my life? The more I thought about it, the more I felt like a normal life after this was impossible. Not unless I found out why Lockwood had kidnapped me.

Mason would come through for me. I didn't know why, but I felt deep in my body that he was going to do everything in his power.

I felt like he was...

He was someone I was supposed to meet. Like it was meant to be.

MASON

I heard Lockwood's light footsteps coming down the stairs half an hour later. It had taken him a while to realize his key was missing. A good thing for me, since I'd needed time to think after Maya refused to come with me. I would've taken her to safety and burned this place down. She would've watched it go up in flames from my truck.

I was still going to do it. It would just have to wait.

Lockwood found me playing with his key, casually rolling it between my fingers. He stopped in front of me, arms crossed over his chest.

"Did you call my boss?" I asked.

"Yes."

"And what did Taros tell you?"

"That you like acting out, but you're loyal."

"Damn straight." I got up.

Lockwood didn't flinch even as I towered over him. His confidence was impressive. I held the key out to him.

"Did you go inside?" he said as he took it and studied it, as if to make sure it was unscratched.

"I did."

He nodded. "Should I call your boss again?"

"What for?"

He lifted an eyebrow and waited for me to elaborate.

"You said she did something to deserve this," I said. "What did she do?"

"Again with the questions," he sighed. "You only need to do your job, guard."

I wasn't going to get anything out of him. It was a useless strategy anyway, since every time he opened his mouth, he was probably lying.

"I have a proposition for you," I said. "You must feed her three times a day. Let me do it and add a weekly bonus to my salary."

Lockwood cocked his head to the side. For a moment, he studied me intensely.

"That would make my life easier," he said, eventually. "I can't trust the housekeeper, you understand. I barely feel comfortable letting her clean your room and bring your meals."

I shrugged. "Figured as much. I can do it for you, make sure she's fed. You won't have to come down here all the time, and you can focus on your work in the lab."

Lockwood pushed his glasses up the bridge of his nose. A habit that had become irritating to me.

"You got a deal," he said. "It would take a lot off my shoulders. I don't like dealing with her. I mean, you went in there, you saw the state of that room. You know what I mean. And she's not the most easy-going creature in the world."

"I'm used to dealing with difficult people," I said.

He held the key up to me. "I have a copy, of course."

I nodded and took it.

"You'll find her dinner in the kitchen at seven. Good luck."

He turned to leave, and I let him take a few steps before stopping him, wanting to make my question sound like an afterthought.

"Can the housekeeper find her some clothes? You're right, I saw the state of her and the room. I can fix it, and I don't need much."

"Fine. Whatever you need."

I waited for him to disappear up the stairs, then I shook my head and started pacing the room again. I needed to calm down. Now that I knew what kind of person he was, his mere presence activated the fire in my belly. The raging one.

Golems didn't feel and express emotions like humans did. Instead of feelings, we had fire that heated us up from the inside. It was as if a sort of alchemy process happened in our bodies as a reaction to what others did or said, or to outside events that were out of our control. The fire started in our belly if we hated someone, and in our heart if we felt pulled toward someone. The fire of the belly was all about rage, defiance and action, and the fire of the heart was about love, compassion and gratitude. The heat radiated through our organs, our muscles and our stone skin, and it could scorch an enemy, or envelop a loved one in soothing warmth.

Lockwood made the worst kind of fire roil inside my belly.

I'd gotten what I wanted from him, though. The key was in my possession, and I could go in and out of Maya's room as I pleased. She needed someone to take care of her, and that was going to be me. There was something about her. Something more than her needing my help because she was innocent. When I'd touched her, she'd stirred the fire of the heart within me. It was for a fleeting moment, but I wondered...

Could it be that she was the one? The woman who could make my fire burn with such passion that it would be impossible to put out? Could she be my mate?

Mates were rare. For golems, it wasn't impossible to find one, but it certainly wasn't a guarantee. My brother hadn't married his fated mate. I knew because he'd told me. The night before his and Kara's wedding, I'd asked him about the fire of the heart, and if she made it burn brightly in his chest. His words were,

"Sometimes, she does. There is heat there, I can feel it. It's undeniable, yet it's not what you'd expect."

"So, she's not the one," I said.

He shook his head. "She doesn't have to make my heart consume itself for me to love her. Those stories about fated mates... Eh. I don't think I believe them anymore, Mason."

It had saddened me that Kara didn't make Goliath's heart explode like fireworks, but maybe my brother was right. Maybe it didn't have to be fireworks or liquid fire to be real and amazing. Seeing him and Kara build a family made me forget about fated mates. They were so rare, anyway. Why would I get one when my brother hadn't? He was just as deserving as me, maybe more.

Now that I'd met Maya just an hour ago, I was feeling differently already. One touch had been enough for me to feel heat in my heart. I couldn't help but wonder...

What would a kiss do?

MAYA

The sound of the key turning in the lock made me startle and scramble to the farthest corner of the room. I let out a breath of relief when I saw it was Mason. Still, I didn't think I could control my reaction the next time. He was bringing me dinner.

"You shouldn't be forced to live like this a second longer," he said. "Tonight, when everyone's asleep, I'll go look for the information you want. And then we're getting out of here."

"Okay."

He placed the tray on the ground and turned to the bucket in the opposite corner from where I was standing. I blushed to the tips of my ears, and when he took it to empty it, I felt like crying. I fixed my gaze on my shoes and didn't look up until he returned. He had two buckets, one empty, the other filled with water, and clean clothes draped over one arm.

"You can wash and change," he said. "If you want, you can use the bathroom in the other room."

"Lockwood might come in at any moment and catch us," I said.

"That's true."

"It's fine. I can make do. Thank you."

"Do you need help?"

I thought about it for a second. I felt weak, and every bone in my body hurt. But I didn't know Mason well enough to let him help me with something that was so vulnerable and intimate. Even though I felt an inexplicable pull toward him, I had to keep a clear head.

"I can manage. Thanks."

"Okay."

He walked out of the room and locked the door. Just in case Lockwood came to see how things were going in his absence. This was the first time he wasn't bringing me food himself.

I washed myself the best I could, changed into the fresh clothes that were a size too big, then knocked on the door when I was done. Mason came in and disposed of the bucket that was now filled with dirty water. I felt like a new person, and even though I was terribly embarrassed that he had to see me like this and take care of me like I was a child, I reminded myself that it wasn't my fault.

Unless Lockwood wasn't lying, and it was...

No, he was surely lying. I didn't feel like I was a bad person. Amnesia or no amnesia, that was something I simply knew.

"Would you like to have dinner together?" Mason asked.

"That would be nice."

He brought his own food, and we sat down on the floor to eat. It was awkward at first. We stole glances at each other, almost furtively, smiling when our eyes met.

"Has more of your memory come back?" he asked.

"Yes. I know where I live. I remember my home address. That's great, right?"

He nodded.

"I remember my parents. They live in a different state. I moved here for college and stayed. I see them once a year, but we call each other all the time. They must be worried sick. They've probably already called the police. I'm not sure how long I've been here. Three days? Four? Less than a week."

"Do you have any siblings?"

I shook my head. "No. Do you?"

"I have a brother."

"What's his name? Tell me about him." This was a good opportunity to get to know Mason better.

"Goliath. He is married to Kara, a human. They have two children, Xavier and Nira."

My eyes widened. "A golem and a human woman? How does that work?" Not that it interested me personally. No... not at all!

He chuckled. "When it's true love, you make it work. They would do anything for each other and for their children. And I would do anything for them."

"No, but I mean... physically. How does it work?"

His eyes widened slightly when he understood what I was talking about.

I blushed. "I'm sorry. I don't mean to pry. It's rude of me to ask such things. I'm just curious. You don't have to tell me."

"No, not at all. I was curious too when my brother brought Kara home and announced she was the one. I had the same question, and he had to explain it to me."

He averted his gaze, and I waited. He seemed to be embarrassed too, which only fueled my curiosity.

"Golems are made of stone," he started. "I mean, our skin is. Not the same stone we find in nature, but very similar. There are a few molecular differences. On the inside, though, we're very much alive. Our organs are similar to yours, we bleed if something pierces our skin and reaches underneath, though that rarely happens. Compared to humans, there's something extra that we have. Fire."

"Fire?"

"Yes. This fire can start in three different places in our bodies." He touched his heart first. "Here." Then his stomach. "Here." Below his stomach, near his pelvis. "And here."

"Incredible. I had no idea!"

"It's something that's specific to my species. Well, the fire that burns in... this area," he motioned at his pelvis again, "Produces a liquid that pours out and into... I mean during... You know." He took a breath and chuckled awkwardly. "I'm sorry. My brother explained it better, but I can't seem to find the words."

"Well, I'm sure your brother could take the liberty of calling things by their name." I laughed.

He laughed with me. "Yes. Anyway, you get it."

"Sort of. Isn't it... hot?"

"A little. Not uncomfortably hot, according to Goliath. And his wife hasn't melted yet, so..."

We laughed harder. The tension dissipated, and I was glad I'd asked him this uncomfortable question. It had brought us closer.

"Right, so," he continued, "We thought this liquid is for lubrication purposes only, but it appears that if a golem does, well... you know what with a human female, the liquid helps... mmm... stretch things? So she can... um... you know, accommodate him?" He rubbed the back of his head. "I'm sorry. I'm sure I could've explained this better."

"No, no! You explained it beautifully!" I couldn't stop laughing and blushing like I had the fire he was talking about inside me, too. "I get it. Trust me. I can almost picture it. The whole process."

He fixed me with his gaze. "You can?"

I bit the inside of my lip. Okay, maybe I shouldn't have said that. Could he tell I was imagining him on top of me, the liquid he'd described dripping from his...

Oh, wow! I needed to get a hold of myself, because I was starting to feel a similar kind of liquid drenching my panties.

He didn't look away from my face, and I wondered... Was he imagining me under him?

"Maybe we should change the subject," I said.

"You're right." He chuckled and looked away. "Yes, let's change the subject."

"So, what's your job, exactly? Are you independent, or..."

"I work for Monster Security Agency. It's private, the agents are all monsters. I guess that's obvious. My brother worked for them too, but then he had an accident and had to retire."

"That's how you ended up guarding me," I said.

"Vincent Lockwood hired me, yes. I didn't know what the job was. I signed a standard contract that only had a few extra clauses. I will confess that it sounded fishy, but I didn't know quite how fishy it could be. He told me I had to stand guard outside the door and not ask questions. Had I behaved, this would've been long term. We both know I'm not behaving, and this ends tonight."

I took a deep breath. "What's the plan? You'll go snooping around?"

"Yes. I'll find whatever I can, then I'm burning this place to the ground, with Lockwood in it. You can't change my mind, Maya."

I smiled. "I don't want to. I just want to know why he did this to me, if what he says about his mother is true... I want to know, that's all. If I am to have a normal life after this, I need closure."

"I understand. I will do everything I can to give you that closure."

I reached out and gently touched his arm. "I know you regret taking this job, but you shouldn't. You're a good guy, Mason."

He shook his head. "I should've done something sooner. The moment I realized he had a person in here. I let him get into my head."

"Don't think like that. I know I don't."

I stretched and yawned, feeling exhausted after the eventful day.

"You should rest," he said, standing up.

He offered me his hand, and I took it. But my legs had fallen asleep, and as soon as I got up, I collapsed. He caught me in his arms and held me against him for a moment. I could feel his stone-like skin radiate heat, and I pressed myself closer to him, trying to feel more of it. It was a strange sensation. As the heat seeped into my body, it soothed all the aches in my muscles.

"Maya," he whispered.

I felt his hot breath on top of my head. He was so tall that I was basically hugging his lower abs.

"Sorry, I'm fine," I said, pulling away.

He let me, and I was a little disappointed. At the same time, he was being careful, respectful of my personal space. That was a good sign that I couldn't ignore.

"I'll help you to the bed."

I laughed. "Bed..."

"Mattress..."

"Thank you, Mason."

"Anything for you, Maya."

MASON

The moment she was in my arms, I knew. She was my mate. The fire in my heart burst with such force that I thought it would become visible through the cracks in my skin. I tried to tame it, push it down, so Maya wouldn't freak out at the sight of it. Fortunately, I was successful. The flame throbbed in my chest, eager to spill out, but I kept it under control.

And then a second fire started in my lower region. In simpler words, in my cock. I became so hard that when Maya pulled away, I let out a little breath of relief. I wanted her in my arms, but not at the cost of scaring her if she felt my erection poke at her ribs.

This was the Mating Fire, and it was even rarer than the fire of the heart. And it wasn't just a little heat in my chest and down there. It was a boiling volcano.

Now I felt even sadder for my brother that he'd never boiled like this for Kara. The fire of the heart could ignite on its own for loved ones, like family and close friends. And the fire of the... um... well, loins?... could be ignited by an intimate partner. But both? At the same time? Only a true mate could do that.

I helped her lie down on the mattress. She let out a groan as her joints popped. My incandescent heart ached for her. She was so thin, even if Lockwood had fed her decently these past few days. The stress was too much for her. I wanted to scoop her into my arms and run away with her. Where would I take her, though? To her house? I didn't trust that she was safe there. To my apartment? Right. I didn't have one anymore. I'd given it up knowing that I would be working for Lockwood long term and living here, in his basement.

Okay, this was something I needed to figure out before I burned down the house with Lockwood in it. The only place I could think of was my brother's house. She would be safe there, with me and my family.

"You're in pain," I said.

"A little."

"What hurts?"

She laughed bitterly. "Everything? My left side is the worst. I think a concussion wasn't the only thing I got when I tried to fight him off."

She lifted her shirt gingerly, and I saw the bruise on her delicate ribs. She probed it with her fingers, wincing.

"You don't think I have a broken rib, do you?"

I pressed my hand to the bruise. My hand was so big that it covered three quarters of the space between her armpit and hip bone. I let my heat seep through, hoping it would soothe her.

"That feels better," she said.

"I don't think anything's broken," I said. "You'd be in much more pain, probably unable to sit or stand."

She smiled. "That's good news."

She closed her eyes, and we stayed like that for a while. My hand on her soft skin felt divine. The heat of her body mingled with mine, and it only intensified the Mating Fire that burned inside me.

When I thought she'd fallen asleep, I removed my hand and stood up.

"Mason?"

"Yes?" Apparently, she was still awake.

"I know you have to execute the plan, but could you stay a while longer? Ten minutes. Please?"

Never in my life was I going to say no to her.

"It's early, anyway," I said. "Lockwood works in his lab until late."

"Perfect, then. Twenty minutes."

"I'll stay for as long as you want, Maya."

MAYA

His warm hand on my ribs made the pain dissipate. Quite literally. His touch was like a soothing balm.

I reached for him and pulled him onto the mattress with me. He was careful not to land on top of me and laid down by my side. I turned to face him. For a long minute, we stared into each other's eyes. His were two dark orbs, but now that I was looking at him so closely, I could see there was a tint of red in them.

"I want you to feel safe," he said, a bit breathlessly.

And that was when I noticed we weren't touching at all. He was lying on his side, facing me, keeping his hands to himself.

"I do feel safe with you," I said, and moved closer to him.

He waited to see what I was going to do. I nestled against him and pulled his arm over me. He was tense at first, but as I pressed my cheek to his rough chest, I felt him relax. I relaxed too, and within minutes, it felt like we'd been made for each other. As crazy as it might have sounded, our bodies fit perfectly together. I closed my eyes and focused on the soothing sounds that seemed to come from deep within his body.

It wasn't just his heartbeat, or the way he breathed softly above my head. There was this low vibration that I could hear if I listened hard enough. Like there was something beneath the surface of his skin that was boiling and bubbling. It was almost like a purr, but not quite. It was hard to explain. All I knew was that it calmed my nerves and put me in a state of mind where it was easy to trust that everything was going to be okay.

Mason held me gingerly, and I soon forgot we were in the filthy basement of a madman. It was just the two of us, and the outside world didn't matter. All the aches in my body vanished, and I felt comfortable and as light as a feather for the first time in days. If not months or years, since it wasn't like I didn't have various pains in my body on a daily basis from sitting too long and not exercising at all. I drifted to sleep.

I dreamed of a flower field. Foxgloves and poppies. I breathed in deeply and felt their fresh scent fill my lungs. I was in the middle of the field, and as I advanced, I could feel them brush against my legs and my arms. I extended my hands and touched the brightly colored petals with my fingers.

Mason stirred. I clung to him harder. He stirred again, and I felt him getting up. I groaned and furrowed my brows, not wanting the flower field to fade. But he was leaving, and I didn't want him to. I let the dream go and cracked an eye open.

"No," I murmured.

"Maya, I need to check if Lockwood went to bed."

"Five more minutes."

He sighed and let me pull him back down. I wrapped my arms around his neck and smashed our bodies together. Before I could overthink it, I pressed my lips to his, and I was surprised at how smooth they were, like polished stone. He let out a surprised grunt and froze. I moved my lips against his, coaxing him to respond. He did so slowly, reluctantly, as if he couldn't believe this was happening, and he didn't want to ruin it by being too eager.

I could tell he wanted me. His body grew even warmer, and I pressed myself flush against him, wanting all that warmth to myself. We kissed for a minute, maybe longer, and the heat intensified, until he was more than warm – he was hot. I couldn't pull away. I didn't want to. He could scorch me, and I wouldn't care.

"Maya," he murmured as he pulled away so we could both breathe.

"I don't know what I'm doing," I said. "But I want this. I want you, Mason. I can't explain it."

"I can, but I..."

I didn't let him finish. I kissed him again, pushing my tongue inside his mouth, tasting him hungrily. After a moment's hesitation, he responded, and our tongues started battling for dominance. I let him win with a moan, practically melting in his arms. I hooked one leg over him and started grinding my hips against him, causing sweet friction right where I needed it most.

"I want to feel something," I whispered against his lips. "I want to feel something good, Mason..."

I continued to rub myself against him. My core throbbed for him, but I knew this wasn't the time and place to take this to the next level. Plus, we'd only just met. Still, I needed some kind of release. I needed to be close to him.

My hand reached between us. I traced the shape of his cock through his pants, marveling at how long and thick it was.

"You don't know what you're doing to me," he said. But he didn't stop me.

I moved my hand lower and cupped his heavy balls, then rubbed the massive length, all the while imagining what it would feel like to have him inside me. I moved my hips more frantically, feeling myself getting closer and closer to the edge. I'd never brought myself to orgasm like that... just by rubbing my clit against a man's leg, like a cat in heat. The simple idea of this action made me blush furiously, but I couldn't stop myself. I needed release, and if I didn't get it, I was going to cry. I was that desperate for it.

"Please," I murmured.

He held me close, his fingers gripping the back of my shirt.

"Anything you want," he whispered in my ear. "Anything you need, Maya."

The way he said my name... I would never get tired of it. His hot breath in my ear was what threw me over the edge. I opened my eyes wide as the orgasm swept me away, and I thought I saw light peeking through the cracks in his skin. I didn't know what it meant. I had no idea how golems worked, aside from what he'd told me. His skin radiated an intense heat that amplified my orgasm, and I let out a cry as I came long and hard.

It took me a minute to recover. He waited patiently, his fingers combing through my hair. When my mind cleared, I let go of him and put some distance between our bodies, so I could look up into his eyes. From dark, they had become completely red.

"I'm sorry," I said. "This is happening fast, I know."

"Never apologize for how you feel."

He placed a kiss on my forehead. I closed my eyes and enjoyed it. When he stood up, I didn't stop him. He straightened his clothes and rolled his shoulders. He was getting ready to do what he'd said he'd do. I wanted him with me, but I also wanted to know why Lockwood had kidnapped me.

"Are you going to be okay?" he asked.

I nodded. "Come back to me."

"Of course I will. We're getting out of here tonight."

I reached up and clung to his sleeve for a second.

"Mason, I'm sorry I dragged you into this. My life's a mess, and I don't even know why. You have a family... Your brother, your niece and nephew... I hope this isn't too dangerous."

He took my hand in his and looked me in the eye.

"I'm the one who's dangerous, Maya. Lockwood has no idea what he got himself into, but he'll soon find out."

"Be careful."

"I won't be long."

With that, he left, and I was once again alone in the basement. He'd left the light on and didn't lock the door. I appreciated it, but I had no intention of leaving here without him. I truly hoped he was more dangerous than my captor, who was, after all, only human. But I knew nothing about Dr. Vincent Lockwood. He'd been able to kidnap me all by himself. However, Mason was a golem. The only reason he hadn't done anything to Lockwood yet was because he'd been hired by him, and he'd wanted to play his cards right, so we could get the information I wanted.

Tonight was going to be a long night, but not longer than the nights of torture Lockwood had put me through.

It was going to end soon. I just needed to hang tight.

MASON

I had to move slowly, which I hated, but considering my height and weight, it was the only way I could be stealthy. To some extent, at least. The house was quiet. I started with the first floor, which I knew well, and as I expected, I didn't find anything. The rooms on this floor were all normal looking, as they were the most frequented by staff and visitors. Nothing shady here. I turned my attention to the stairs, which led to the second floor and above, wondering if they were going to creak under my massive weight. I was going to have to be extra-careful and have a story ready in case I ran into Lockwood.

Though, at this point, I was tired of telling stories. I was tired of pretending. If Lockwood had the misfortune of finding me snooping, my Plan B was to immobilize him, make him tell me what I needed to know, and then tie him up to a chair, like he'd done so many times to Maya.

The stairs did creak a little, but I managed to make my way to the second floor with no incidents. Every five seconds, I stopped to listen to the sounds of the mansion. The second floor presented me with too many doors to my liking. I had to be vigilant and choose wisely. The last thing I needed was to barge into Lockwood's private quarters.

I opened one door, and it was a bedroom. Empty. The bed was neatly made, so I guessed it must have been a guest bedroom. I opened another door, praying Lockwood wasn't sleeping inside, but it was just another empty room. Okay, so it seemed like the second floor was all bedrooms. The smart thing to do was to advance to the third floor and see what was there. Once again, I braved the stairs, one step at a time, moving as gingerly as I could.

The third floor was more airy and seemed to be divided differently than the second floor. The doors weren't all the same, and when I opened the first one, I found myself in a library that was filled with books. It was grander than the one on the first floor, and if that one had fiction books on its shelves, this one only had biology and chemistry books. I lost interest easily and moved to the next door.

Jack pot. I'd found Lockwood's lab. As I walked between the tables, my eyes raking over the glass hardware and machines I had never seen before, I willed the fire that burned in my belly to grow brighter, so it would illuminate the room better. In the dark, I didn't need artificial light. I could use my own fire to see. I found tubes filled with blood, and I knew it was Maya's. That only made my fire burn stronger.

At the back of the lab, there was a door. I opened it and found myself in a study. There was a huge mahogany desk, leather armchairs and a leather sofa. My intuition told me this was the place I'd been looking for. I rounded the desk and started pulling out the drawers. Sure enough, they were filled with files and stray documents. I gathered them and placed them on the desk, and as I sank into the chair, I started going through them.

I didn't have time to read them all. I didn't care for Lockwood's research, and I only looked for Maya's name. Maya Lucas. I rummaged through files and papers until I found a rather thick file with her name on it. With trembling hands, I opened it, feeling slightly sick to my stomach, not knowing what I would read inside.

Lockwood had accused Maya of having done something to his mother. Since Maya still suffered from partial amnesia because of the concussion he'd given her, the question of whether he was lying or not still lingered. I went over the first page in the file, which contained general information about Maya. Name, age, address, job, blood type, and a few other details. The next few pages were dedicated to her family, which I found odd. There was a family tree, and I traced it with my finger, reading out the names in a low voice, trying to pay attention to who these people they were to Maya. As she'd told me, she didn't have any siblings. However, she had cousins, aunts and uncles. The family tree went all the way to her great-great-great grandparents, and the name of her great-great-great-grandfather was circled with red. He had a pretty odd name – Korin Lowcastle. Fancy. It didn't sound particularly American or... human, for that matter. But what did I know?

I turned a few more pages, and to my surprise, they weren't about Maya anymore. Suddenly, the focus of the file was this Korin Lowcastle guy who was her ancestor, and his daughter – Julie. Julie Graves. Obviously, I asked myself... Why did his daughter take the name of her mother, and not the name of her father? The answer came when I turned the page and read that Korin had mysteriously disappeared from his family's life right after she was born.

I turned a few more pages. As I began to make sense of what this whole thing meant, I felt sicker and sicker to my stomach. Maya had done nothing to deserve her fate. It was all about her family and who her great-great-great-grandfather was.

I heard a creak outside the study, and I stilled. Shuffling footsteps in the lab told me I wasn't alone anymore. I closed the file, stood up, and tucked it in the back of my jeans. Just as I rounded the desk, the intruder appeared in the doorway. Though, to be fair, I was the intruder here.

It was a woman. She looked old and frail, with hair that was completely white, but with a face so young that it gave me pause. It was as if one half of my brain told me she was old, and the other insisted she couldn't be older than thirty.

"You're the bodyguard," she said.

I wasn't sure how to play this. I decided to be as monosyllabic as possible and hope she would do the talking.

"Yes, ma'am."

"What are you doing here?"

I stared at her and refused to answer, curious what reaction that would elicit. She stepped inside the study and looked around. She noticed the files on the desk, let out a sigh, then closed her eyes for a moment. When she opened them again, she seemed sad. Resigned.

"You must think I'm a horrible person," she said.

I cocked my head to the side. Great. She was talking.

"You must think I'm exactly like my son. I'm not. I never wanted this. But there's no saying no to Vincent. There's no changing his mind when something gets into his head."

My eyes widened slightly. This was Lockwood's mother! How could she be so young? And still... feel so old? The vibe she gave off felt unnerving. Like there was something about her that wasn't quite right. Clearly, she was human, but humans didn't give off such vibes.

"It's gotten out of control, you know. I keep telling Vincent this has to stop. He has to put an end to it. I've already lived way beyond what God intended." She paused, sighed, and studied her hands. "I used to be religious. Now I can't pray anymore. It wouldn't be right." She looked up at me. "Tell me, what's the new girl like? I know he has her in the basement. What's her name?"

"Maya Lucas."

She nodded. "What does she look like?"

"Brown hair and blue eyes."

"The girl before her had red hair and green eyes. She must've been a beauty. Vincent never lets me see them, says he doesn't want me to get attached."

I felt the fire in my belly boil harder, stronger, bigger. I calmed it down with cold, calculated thoughts.

"What's your name?" she asked.

"Mason."

She wiped her palms on her long, sensible skirt, which was black and made of wool, then curled her hands into shaking fists at her sides.

"Mason, I must confess something to you. I don't want Maya to end up like the last one. It would be the last straw. I'm already dead on the inside, though I'm alive and healthy on the outside. I shouldn't be. It's all upside down. See, I was diagnosed with cancer very young. Vincent was only fifteen. I did all the treatments under the sun, and I held off for his sake. He needed me. But in the end, I couldn't be cured, and that was something we both had to accept. I made my peace with it, but Vincent refused to let me die. Since he was a child, he's studied biology, chemistry, and medicine with passion. When I first told him I had cancer, he started looking for a cure. I let him because I thought it was his way of coping. I never thought he would find a cure. But he did. Unfortunately, it was at the expense of other people's lives."

Her story corroborated what I'd read in Maya's file. It all made sense.

"Tell me something," I said. "Did Maya do anything to you? Did she hurt you?"

Her eyebrows lifted like I'd just said something that shook her entire world.

"No. Never. Who told you that? Vincent? Oh, he would say anything... I've never even met Maya. I told you, he never lets me see them. If anything,

Maya is helping me. Her blood is the reason I look so young." She touched her face and winced. "When I look in the mirror, I see no wrinkles, and it's uncanny. Oh, how I wish my face showed my true age. I don't recognize myself. More than that, how I wish my son would just let me go. I know I was never supposed to live this long. I can feel it."

"What do you want me to do?" I asked.

"What you must." Her tone turned grave, and she looked me straight in the eye with slightly furrowed brows. "I'll never forgive myself if Maya ends up like the last one. Like the ones before her. Vincent's study is off limits, so I know you're not here because he asked you to bring him something. He's asleep in his bedroom on the second floor. You're here because you know what's been happening in this house all these years, and you want to stop it."

I nodded. She was wise if she could read me so easily.

"So, do what you must, Mason, and do it fast."

"What about you?" I asked.

She smiled bitterly. "Don't worry about me. I've been a prisoner, just like the girls in the basement. You know what?" She looked out the window.

"What a beautiful night. I think I'll take my old Chevy out for a ride to the beach. I haven't driven in so long, I miss it."

I shook my head. This was taking a turn I had not expected.

"Without the blood transfusions, how long will you live?" I asked.

She shrugged. "Who knows? I might get two weeks, I might get a month. I'll make the best of it. That's all I wish, Mason. To be rid of this house, of the knowledge that the basement is never empty, and to be rid of... him. I wish to take long walks on the beach every day, catch every sunset and every sunrise."

"But he's your son."

"Hm. He's changed. His obsession with keeping me alive has changed him."

I wanted to say something else, but she raised a hand to stop me.

"No more questions. You've got more answers than you thought you'd be getting tonight. I have a long drive ahead of me if I want to catch the sunrise on the beach. For once, Vincent won't bring me back by force. I trust you to make sure of that."

She turned and left. I stood there, stunned, trying to wrap my head around everything I'd learned. After five minutes, I snapped out of it and told myself I'd have time to think about it later.

Maya was waiting for me.

MAYA

I heard Mason's footsteps thundering down the stairs, and I jumped to my feet. I wrapped my arms around myself and stared at the door, knowing it was unlocked, but also knowing that I didn't have the courage to march over to it, open it, and meet him halfway. It was as if Lockwood had damaged me so deeply that I couldn't even save myself anymore.

Mason barged in, and the first thing I noticed was the way he was glowing. It was as if a fire was burning inside him, so bright and powerful that it spilled through his skin. I saw actual flames lick the surface of his skin, and his eyes were aglow.

"What's going on?" I asked.

"We have to go now."

"Did you get..."

"Yes. We have to go now, Maya."

He closed the distance between us and scooped me up into his arms. I clung to him as he rushed out the door and up the stairs to the first floor.

I smelled smoke. As he ran through corridor after corridor, the smoke became denser. I felt my eyes starting to sting and water. How big was this house? All I'd seen of it was the basement. I took in the sparkling chandelier in the main hall, and when I looked at the stairs that led to the next floor, I saw flames licking the walls.

"What did you do?" I asked.

"I told you I was going to burn this place to the ground."

"I didn't think you meant literally."

He opened the front door, and we were out in the fresh air, finally. It was dark, and he crossed the lawn toward a truck that was waiting in the driveway. It was massive, as big as a tank, so I concluded it must have been Mason's car, since no human would need such a big and clunky means of transportation. As he ran, I clung to him more tightly and looked over his shoulder.

The mansion was impressive. Under the moonless sky, it was ablaze. The fire had started on the top floor.

"What happened to Lockwood?" I asked.

"In his room, sleeping. I made sure to block the door, so he can't get out."

I didn't know how to feel about that. Dr. Vincent Lockwood had kidnapped me and kept me either cuffed or tied up for days. He'd drawn my blood after giving me a concussion and effectively erasing my memory for God knew how long. I was better, but I still had gaps. Did I think he deserved to die? Yes. Did that mean I could stomach the fact that he was about to be burned alive?

I hid my head in Mason's chest and closed my eyes. He was so warm, his heat so soothing, thrumming from within him as if its sole purpose was to bring me peace and make me feel safe. I never wanted him to let me go.

We reached his truck, and he set me back on my feet. He threw the passenger door open, then helped me inside. It was so high that it would've been a challenge for me to climb in on my own. He rushed to the driver's side and got in.

"Are you okay?" he asked.

"Yes."

As he started the engine, I couldn't look away from the burning mansion. The flames had engulfed the second and the first floors.

"Should we call 911?" I asked.

"Absolutely not. Let it all turn to ashes."

"I don't know, Mason..."

He turned to me and forced me to look at him. "Listen to me, Maya. Do you know what I found out? That you're not the first one. There were other women, and God knows what happened to them. And you wouldn't have been the last."

I shuddered. "Okay."

"Okay."

I looked back at the house. No matter how hard it was for me to witness the fire, it was impossible to look away. I tried to make sense of my feelings, but it was all happening too fast. I was conflicted. There had been other women. Vincent Lockwood certainly deserved to die a horrible death.

As Mason started pulling out of the driveway, I saw one of the garage doors open. A red Chevy shot out, straight to the gates that were opening before it, as if someone had activated them by remote control.

"Who is that? Is that Lockwood?"

Mason hesitated for a moment. We watched together as the red Chevy drove through the gates, leaving them open for us.

"No," he said. "That's his mother."

"What?!"

"Victoria Lockwood."

"So, she's alive. I never did anything to her."

"No. That was Lockwood gaslighting and manipulating both of us. If anything, you helped Victoria."

"How?"

He drove the truck through the gates, and we were on our way to the main road. I realized the mansion was isolated. There was not a neighbor in sight. It was going to take a while before someone saw the fire and called 911. It would be too late. The house would probably be ashes by then. No one was going to know what had happened in that basement.

"I'll tell you everything when we get to my brother's place."

"Your brother's place?"

"It will be safe for you there. I know you want to go home, Maya, but I'll feel better knowing you're with me."

"Okay. Thank you."

He reached over and squeezed my hand.

"Get some sleep," he said. "Let me take care of everything."

"I'm worried," I confessed. "What if they figure out it was you who started the fire?"

"One step at a time."

"What if you're in danger now?"

He looked at me. "Maya, I can take care of myself. And I will take care of you. Do you trust me?"

I bit the inside of my cheek, hesitating. Not that I didn't trust him. I didn't trust the authorities to understand what had happened at the mansion and in that basement. And I'd just seen Victoria Lockwood, my captor's mother, escape in a red Chevy. She was an eyewitness, and Mason had done nothing to stop her.

"I trust you," I said.

He smiled at me, and like the heat of his body, his smile warmed me down to my core. I relaxed and let my head fall against the seat. It was so big that it was almost like a single bed.

I closed my eyes and drifted to sleep.

MASON

The sun was up when we arrived at my brother's house. The children were having breakfast as Kara prepared their backpacks for kindergarten. I felt bad for interrupting their routine and bringing chaos into their peaceful household, but this was the only place where I was certain Maya would be safe. For a while, at least, until things calmed down, and we knew where we stood.

Goliath opened the door when he heard me pulling up into the driveway. He smiled and waved when he saw me get out of the truck. I nodded at him and went to the passenger's side to get Maya. She was too tired to walk, and even if her initial reaction was to protest needing help, I took her in my arms and carried her to the house. At the sight of her – more specifically, the state she was in – Goliath's smile faded. He moved out of the doorway to let us through.

"Good God, what happened?" Kara came running from the kitchen, kids in tow. "You poor thing, are you okay? Come, lie down on the couch."

She didn't know who Maya was, yet didn't hesitate to adopt her in an instant. It was just the type of person my brother's wife was – warm-hearted and compassionate.

"I'm okay," Maya chuckled, trying to sound brave. "I've been worse."

She was shaking all over, and it dawned on me that she was just starting to process everything she'd been through. Being stuck in that basement had disconnected her from the world and from the normalcy of it, and now that she was surrounded by people again – Kara being human and her two kids hybrids – she was being hit by the realization that what had happened to her was completely and irreparably wrong. Her chin trembled and her eyes filled with tears. She quickly swiped at them with the back of her sleeve.

"Do you think I could take a bath?" she asked.

"Oh my God, of course. Anything you need. Here, I'll help you up."

Kara hooked an arm around Maya's waist, and together, they ambled upstairs. Since my brother had lost his leg, they'd done work on the house, and now he and Kara lived downstairs, while the whole second floor was Xavier's and Nira's. I was grateful Kara had taken Maya to the upstairs bathroom because that meant I could have a real conversation with Goliath before I had to show Maya the file I'd taken from Lockwood's study.

"Does this mean we're not going to kindergarten today?" Xavier asked, hope twinkling in his dark eyes.

"Absolutely not," my brother said. "I will take you right now. Are you all packed up?"

The children groaned but went to get their backpacks.

"Ten minutes," Goliath said to me. "There's coffee in the kitchen."

I nodded. I was grateful to have ten minutes to myself, to think about everything that had happened and anticipate what consequences I might have to suffer. When my brother returned, I'd have to break it to him I'd just burned down my client's house with him inside it. And I needed him and his family to be my alibi. Involving them in this was selfish of me, but what other choice did I have? Maya was my mate. Every time we touched, my body and my soul burned for her. I only hoped my brother would understand that.

I poured coffee into a mug and sat at the kitchen table. From here, I could see the driveway and pretty far down the street. Upstairs, I heard Kara run this way and that, probably retrieving towels and other things Maya needed. I took out the file and placed it on the table. I'd read it all and knew the most important details by heart. Maya had been through so much already, and I hated I had to give this file to her and disrupt her life even more. On the one hand, she would find out things about herself and her family that she'd never even imagined, but on the other hand, I knew that knowledge would change her forever.

I saw my brother's truck pull up next to mine. The fact that he was in a wheelchair didn't stop him from doing most of the things he'd done before, and he didn't like getting help when he didn't ask for it, so I patiently waited for him. When he'd needed to adapt his truck to accommodate the wheelchair, I'd insisted to finance it. We had a huge fight, and in the end, we went fifty-fifty. Above all, Goliath was proud. I couldn't blame him, since I was proud too, and if I sometimes had to fight him to make him accept my help, I was happy to do it.

"Coffee?" I asked as he entered the kitchen.

"Sure." He eyed the file as I poured him a cup. "What's this?"

I ignored his question for now.

"Goliath, what I'm going to ask of you is huge. Before I do it, I need to tell you that Maya is my mate. She has stirred the Mating Fire within me."

"Maya is the girl?"

"Yes."

"Brother, you have a lot of explaining to do. Where did you find her?"

It didn't escape me that he didn't seem happy for me. I was sure it wasn't envy, but just the fact that he could tell I was about to put him in a difficult situation.

"I was hired to guard her by the madman who kidnapped her and locked her up in his basement. It was wrong, and you know me. I won't betray my morality for money. And then I discovered she is my mate, and I burned that place to the ground, with the madman in it. There was no other way."

"The madman who hired you. You killed a client of Monster Security Agency." He shook his head. There was no anger in his voice. No disappointment either. It was more like he was in awe of my choice. "You're done, Mason. This time, for real. You'll never work again. Not in this field."

"I don't care. She's all that matters to me."

"Not if you can't provide for her." There was sadness in his voice this time, and I knew why. He thought he couldn't provide for Kara anymore.

"I'll find a way. I don't give up easily, and neither should you."

"What happens now? Why did you bring her here?"

I rubbed the back of my head. "This job was supposed to be long-term and live-in. I gave up my apartment and put my things in storage. Not that I have a lot to my name." On second thought, what if he was right and I really couldn't provide for Maya? "I didn't want to take her to her place because I don't know if she'll be safe there."

"Her captor is dead."

"I have a feeling there's more to this story than we can see at the moment."

"Like what?"

I shrugged. "I don't know. It's just a hunch. It's like a piece of the puzzle is missing."

"Okay. Well, you're welcome here, of course. Stay for as long as you need. You can use our bedroom upstairs." He thought for a moment. "Is that what you wanted to ask me? It's not that huge of a favor."

I cringed. "No, that's not it. I need an alibi. The police will investigate the fire, and they won't be able to tell what started it."

He grinned. "You started it."

"Not needing gasoline and a match makes starting fires easy." I shook my head at my own misplaced sarcasm. "I erased Maya's traces. They won't know she was ever there. It's best that they don't, so they don't involve her. After everything, she deserves to be left alone. But there will be evidence that I was hired by Lockwood. All they have to do is call the MSA. So, I'm going to need you to say that I was here, with you and your family. That I had the day off and I spent it with you."

"You got it." He didn't even hesitate, and I could just hug him and kiss him. I didn't do it, knowing he would've punched me. "I'll talk to Kara and the kids. We'll get our stories straight. Is that it?"

"Yes. Thank you, brother."

He laughed. "Did you think I would say no?"

"It's a huge ask."

"Between brothers, nothing is a huge ask."

We finished our coffee, and I offered to make more. As I was filling the coffeemaker with water, I heard the girls coming down the stairs. A few seconds later, they were in the kitchen. I turned to look at them, and when I saw Maya, my heart skipped a beat.

She was gorgeous. Freshly bathed, with her damp hair falling down her back, full lips as rosy as her flushed cheeks, and her blue eyes brighter than ever – she was a sight to behold. For the first time, I noticed the discreet splatter of freckles on her slightly upturned nose. Kara had lent her a pair of jeans and a shirt, and even though they were a size bigger, I could tell they were covering the most beautiful body I'd ever seen on a woman, human or not.

"How are you feeling?" I asked.

"So much better."

"You look good." She cocked an eyebrow at me, and I added quickly, "I mean, you look amazing."

She laughed. "Thank you. I feel like a whole new person."

"Coffee?"

"Yes, please!"

She sat down, and Kara went to rummage through the fridge. "I'm making everyone breakfast," she declared. "Don't even think of saying you're not hungry."

No one protested. I, for one, loved my sister-in-law's cooking.

Maya stole a glance at Goliath. I could tell she was curious about his condition, but too polite to ask.

"Goliath worked for Monster Security Agency a long time ago," I said.

Her eyes widened.

"Yeah," Goliath said. "Then I lost a leg, and they had no use for me anymore."

"I'm so sorry."

He shrugged. "Sometimes the worst things happen to you. In this case, me. Nothing I can do about it but move on."

"It's a terrible thing," she said.

We all nodded and were silent for a while, the only sound the clattering of pots and dishes as Kara made breakfast. To break the silence – and because it made no sense to postpone – I pushed the file toward Maya.

"This is what you wanted. Everything's in here."

She inhaled sharply, then exhaled as she placed her fingers on the edges of the file. "The reason Lockwood kidnapped me?"

"That and much more."

"Did you read it?"

"Yes."

"Okay. That's okay."

She opened it, and her own name, along with a copy of her ID, stared at her. As she started reading, I studied her face. She was incredible. My mate. I couldn't have wished for a better woman.

MAYA

The more I read, the more I remembered about myself and my life before Lockwood had knocked me unconscious and given me a concussion. It all came back to me. My memory was intact once again, and I let out a breath of relief. I knew who I was, and I knew I was innocent. I'd always been innocent.

However, it hadn't been "wrong place, wrong time". Dr. Vincent Lockwood had targeted me for a very specific reason, and as the file revealed it to me, the words became blurry, and I realized my eyes were filled with tears. Kara passed a box of paper tissues to me, and I wiped my eyes and my cheeks.

"Are you okay?" Mason asked.

I shook my head. "I don't know. This is all too much. And hard to believe."

"It's true, though. The world is full of hybrids."

Relationships between monsters and humans weren't the norm, but there were no laws against them. Apparently, there had been such a union in the history of my family, as shown by the meticulous family tree Lockwood had made. My great-great-great-grandfather, Korin Lowcastle, had been a vampire. Was, in fact. Yes. Was a vampire, since vampires were immortal.

I didn't know anything about him. No one in my family had ever mentioned him, and it was the first time I even came across his name. A note at the bottom of the page said that Korin vanished from my great-great-great-grandmother's life when she became pregnant, and never returned. He'd abandoned her and their baby. My great-great-great-grandmother married a human man, and together, they had two more children.

Apparently, the offspring of a vampire and a human was called a dhampir, and my great-great-grandmother was one. She had some vampiric traits but was mostly human. The next generations had even less vampiric traits, to the point where they were negligible. In my case, they were basically non-existent, which made me almost a hundred percent human.

Almost, because there was something in my blood. Something Dr. Vincent Lockwood had had a use for.

"This is a lot to take in," I said. "So, my blood, because it's so diluted, can heal a human temporarily and prolong their life without turning them into a vampire. Because I'm not a vampire."

"That's right," Mason said. "Your blood has healing properties. Lockwood's mother has cancer. This was the cure he'd found for her. Vampire blood is too strong, and it would've turned her, had he used it for transfusions. Dhampir blood is also too strong. He had to find someone whose blood was diluted enough but still had the properties needed to keep the disease at bay."

"These people must be rare," Goliath said.

Mason nodded. "I'd think so. Though Maya was not Lockwood's first victim. He's been giving his mother transfusions for years."

"So, I'm rare," I said. "And my reward for being rare was getting kidnapped and basically tortured."

They all looked at me with deep sadness in their eyes. I didn't want them to pity me, and I knew this was not what was happening. I was grateful I wasn't alone. I'd just met Kara and Goliath, but somehow, I didn't perceive them as strangers. They were Mason's family, and Mason was... special to me. There was something between us I couldn't describe or explain. All I knew was that it was powerful, and I wouldn't have had it any other way.

To survive this, I needed Mason. He was my rock. Quite literally, though this wasn't a great time for golem jokes.

I finished reading the file, then closed it. I placed my hands on the cover and took a couple of deep, calming breaths.

"Oh, wow. Um... I don't know what to say. This doesn't change anything. It doesn't change me... who I am..."

"Of course not," Mason said. "Maya, you are perfect. You're the most incredible person I've ever met, and you're so strong. It doesn't matter who your ancestors were."

"A vampire and a dhampir in my family tree," I said. Maybe if I repeated it often enough, I'd eventually wrap my head around it. "I wish my great-great-great-grandmother had never met Korin Lowcastle. He ruined her life. And mine."

Kara reached out and squeezed my arm. "Relationships between humans and monsters aren't a walk in the park, that's for sure. But that's no excuse to leave the woman who's pregnant with your baby. That was selfish and horrible."

"I don't know anything about vampires," I said.

"They're elusive," Mason said. "Because of their dietary preferences, they often live outside the law. They move from one place to another, never settle down."

"I don't know any vampires," Goliath said.

I nodded. "Just as well. I want to detach myself from this whole thing. I am human, and I'll always be human."

Kara started setting the table, and that snapped me out of my thoughts. I offered to help, but she refused. Her husband helped her, though, and before long, we had a rich breakfast before us. Mason dug in with gusto, complimenting Kara's cooking every five minutes, and the laughter and small talk helped me relax and enjoy the food.

I had to call my parents, I thought. I wondered where my phone was. Lockwood must have destroyed it. I didn't know my parents' number by heart, so I'd have to find another way to reach them. I needed a laptop with a Wi-Fi connection. I wanted them to know that I was okay, but I couldn't tell them what had happened to me. One, that would complicate things, and two, I didn't think I had the strength to relive it. I would have to come up with something.

This was stressing me out, so I forced myself to not think about it and just focus on what was in front of me. First, I needed to take care of myself. I needed to rest, come up with a solid strategy, and then execute it.

"Something's still bugging me, though," I said.

Mason, Goliath, and Kara looked at me.

"Okay, he kidnapped me. But why did he hire you?" I fixed Mason with my gaze. "It wasn't like I could escape that godforsaken basement. He was keeping me cuffed to a bolt in the floor. What did he hire you for?"

Mason thought for a moment. "I only talked to his mother for a few minutes, and she told me there had been other victims. She said she didn't want you to end up like them. But I don't know what she meant."

Kara squeezed my arm again. "Maya, it's good you escaped. I'm so glad Mason brought you here. You're safe."

I gave her a grateful smile. "You're right. I'm just... tired." I looked at my plate and realized I couldn't take another bite. "This has been so tasty. I'm full."

"Do you need to lie down?" Kara asked.

"I think so." I looked at Mason. "Can you take me upstairs?"

He jumped to his feet, as if I'd given him an order.

"I'll carry you," he said.

I laughed as I got up, albeit not as energetically as he had. "I can walk, Mason. You've carried me a lot, don't you think?"

"I will carry you anywhere, and for the rest of my life."

His words triggered a pleasant tingling inside my stomach.

MASON

She walked to the stairs by herself, and I followed her close behind. I couldn't take my eyes off her enticing hips as they swayed. She stumbled on the first step, and I rushed to catch her. She laughed, but I frowned and scooped her up into my arms. I was going to carry her to the bedroom, whether she liked it or not.

"Maybe I did it intentionally," she joked, nuzzling my neck.

"Maybe you're too exhausted to see straight."

"No, I'm feeling better. I promise." She pressed herself against me and whispered in my ear, "When I'm so close to you, I really do feel better. I don't know why. I can't explain it."

The Mating Fire started burning within me. My cock grew hard in my pants, and now it was difficult for me to focus on climbing the stairs safely.

"I love this sound you're making all the time," she said. "It's like it comes from inside you. Is it a purr? It sounds like a purr. Like you're a big cat, except you're not."

"That's my fire," I said.

Finally, we reached the second floor. I took her into the bedroom that used to be Kara's and Goliath's. It was spacious, with its own bathroom. There were fresh sheets on the bed, courtesy of my sister-in-law. I gently lay Maya on the bed.

"Stay with me," she said, clinging to me, like she'd done in the basement.

I couldn't resist her, and I had no intention of trying. I climbed in next to her, and she immediately curled up in my arms.

"I feel such a strange pull toward you," she said. "Do you feel it too?"

"Yes. The fire you ignite inside me differs from anything I've felt before. It's called the Mating Fire, and few golems are lucky to experience it. It can only be awakened by a true mate."

She looked up at me, brows slightly furrowed. "What do you mean by true mates?"

"Fated mates." I kissed her lips gently. "You were made for me, and I was made for you. It's clearer to me because I was built to recognize it, but I believe some humans believe in soulmates, too."

"I guess so. I never thought about it."

"You're mine, Maya. I know it with such conviction that I feel myself melting just thinking about it."

"Melting in a good way, I hope," she gave me a playful smile.

I shifted our positions, so I was hovering above her. Our eyes locked, and I found I couldn't look away from her. I wanted to drink her in, have her face imprinted on my soul. I ran my fingers through her hair, and she moaned.

"I was feeling tired earlier," she said, "But I think I'm good now."

"Are you sure?"

"Touch me, Mason. Show me how a golem and a human can be together, fit together perfectly."

Her words made my fire burn brighter. Beneath me, she was illuminated by my warm, red glow. I touched her face, traced her lips with the tips of my fingers, moved down to her beautiful neck and delicate clavicle. She closed her eyes and exhaled, her lips parting with a tremble.

"I will do anything for you, Maya."

Slowly, I started peeling off her clothes. She sat up when I needed her to, lifted her hips so I could roll her jeans down her smooth, pale legs. Her breasts were round and firm, with dark pink nipples that turned into hard pebbles as I fixed my gaze on them. I took in every inch of her body. It hurt my soul that I could see her ribs, knowing she was so thin because of the suffering she'd endured the past several days. I swore to myself that I was going to take care of her, provide for her, and make sure she had everything she needed and more.

"Please," she whispered. "Stop teasing."

I removed my own clothes, throwing them on the floor. She stared at me with wide eyes, her gaze traveling down my chest and abs. When she saw my erect cock for the first time, she gasped.

"Don't worry," I said. "I will be gentle."

She nodded. "I trust you."

MAYA

His touch ignited something inside me. I felt my core throb with need, and no matter how hard I tried to control myself, my body kept shuddering and shaking. I wasn't feeling cold; on the contrary. He radiated so much heat that I was feeling beads of sweat gather at the roots of my hair.

The sight of his cock should've made me reconsider my desire for him, but it only turned me on more. It looked like perfectly polished stone, aside from the tiny cracks through which the Mating Fire that burned beneath his skin peeked. I reached out my hand and touched it. My fingers brushed the smooth length, and Mason let out a groan. His cock was hot, barely a few degrees below burning.

I'd never known golems had such a strong connection with fire, to the point where it literally started within them and burst to the surface.

"If you've changed your mind," he said, hesitantly.

I was mesmerized by his cock, and he was taking it the wrong way. There was nothing that I wanted more than for him to fill me and pour his fire within me. I could only hope I'd be able to withstand it. If it was true that I was his fated mate, then this was going to be the greatest experience of my life. I couldn't wait to belong to him.

"Never," I breathed out. "I want you, Mason."

"I want you, too."

"Then what are you waiting for?"

Without another word, he moved down my body and took hold of my hips. He made me open my legs for him, and he settled between them. I felt his hot breath on my soaked pussy.

His tongue on my clit felt divine. I grabbed onto the sheets and let out a long moan. Instinctively, my thighs tightened around his head, trapping him there, where I needed him most. He traced a line from my clit to my entrance and pushed his tongue inside me. It was as if warmth poured out of his mouth and into my body, and I trembled with pleasure. It was so different from anything I'd ever felt before. It was intense, almost primordial. It was hard to describe.

All I could do was shut off my brain and allow myself to feel it.

He returned to my clit and started tracing circles around it, holding my pussy lips open with two fingers. He licked me until I was a moaning mess, then sucked the bundle of nerves between his lips, driving me almost insane. I was careful to keep as silent as I could since we weren't alone in the house. At the back of my mind, there was this thought that I was being disrespectful to my hosts – two people who had no reason to welcome me like this into their home. But I needed this so badly. After everything I'd been through, I needed to feel this. I needed to feel good, and loved, and wanted.

So, I put it out of my mind. I focused solely on Mason and what his mouth was doing to me. He pressed his tongue to my clit, and that made me forget all my worries. He went back to circling it, faster this time, pushing me closer and closer to release. I let go of the sheets and placed my hands on his head. There was no hair I could grab onto, but that was fine. I'd never thought I'd be into bald men, so these past few days had certainly been filled with surprises.

"There, right there," I whispered. "Please."

I was so close... He didn't stop, didn't slow down, and when he pushed one finger inside my pussy, I arched my back and came unexpectedly. From chasing an orgasm, it simply came crashing through me, taking me by surprise, making me curl my toes and moan a little louder than I probably should have.

"Oh, God... Fuck! Mason... fuck..."

He licked me lazily until my body stopped shaking, then lifted his head and grinned at me.

"You're delicious."

"Let me see how delicious..." I pulled him up and crashed my lips against his.

"I need to be inside you," he murmured as he devoured my mouth like he'd just devoured my pussy. "Now, Maya. Will you let me take you?"

"Yes. Don't ask. Just do it."

I reached between our bodies and ran my fingers up and down his cock. I couldn't get enough of how smooth and warm it felt. I spread my legs wide and guided him to my entrance.

"We mustn't rush," he said. "Let me fill you with my warmth first. It will get you ready."

I remembered what he'd told me about golems and humans mating. There was no way he would fit inside me, so I was glad there was a natural solution to it. It was hard for me to believe that the hot liquid he was going to pour into me was going to stretch me enough to accommodate him, but I could only hope. I didn't understand how it worked, but maybe I didn't have to.

Trust the process. Trust him. And I did.

I felt him push the tip in. It was just two or three inches, and I already felt like he was stretching me a lot. He was thick, not just long, his girth so impressive that to cover it, I'd have to wrap both hands around it.

"I'm sorry," he said, when he felt me squirm a little. "I don't want you to be in pain."

"I'm not."

The truth was that his heat had the same effect on me as in the basement, when he'd put a hand on my bruised ribs and taken the pain away. It was as if he'd healed me. Apparently, I was not the only one with healing powers.

I felt hot liquid drip, drip, drip inside me, and I opened my eyes wide and stared at him in awe. I hadn't thought it was possible.

"How does that feel?" he asked.

"Amazing. I don't even know how you're doing it."

He smiled. "It's a golem thing, I guess. Are you ready for more?"

"Yes, give me more."

A rush of heat filled me, and it was as if a dam had broken. The liquid traveled deep inside me, and Mason penetrated me a few more inches. I didn't feel any pain. I knew he was stretching me, but it didn't feel uncomfortable, or like it was too much.

"Don't stop," I said.

"It's working. I can feel you, Maya. You're opening up for me."

He pushed his cock deeper, and I gasped and panted. It felt incredible. One more thrust, and he was sheathed completely, his heavy balls resting against my buttocks. I'd seen them earlier. They were perfectly round and smooth, two rocks with no hair and no imperfections.

"I don't think I can hold back," he said. His face looked slightly pained. "You feel so good. I just need to... I have to fill you with my seed."

"Well, what have you been filling me with?"

He chuckled nervously. "Lubricant. But I will give you my seed now, my mate."

That made me shake with anticipation. I didn't even care we weren't using protection. This felt right. This man had saved me, had burned a house down to avenge me, and the way I felt about him was overwhelming. I only wanted to be his. The fact that Kara and Goliath were happy together and had two beautiful children confirmed that this was not a mistake. On the contrary, this was what I'd been waiting for all these years, drifting from disappointing relationship to disappointing relationship. When I looked into Mason's eyes, I saw... forever.

He pulled out until only the tip was in, then thrust deep inside me. He should've shattered me in two by now, but he didn't even hit my cervix. He'd literally changed my anatomy, and it blew my mind how my body fit his like a glove. He did it again, and again, until he built a rhythm that promised to push us both over the edge. I tried to meet him halfway by moving my hips upwards. He grabbed me by the hips and lifted me, tucking his knees underneath me. I wrapped my legs around him and let him take control completely. I was half on the bed, half off the bed. He held me like my weight was nothing to him.

"You're so beautiful," he said. "You're mine. I want to see you naked all the time."

"I'm yours," I said.

That, to my ears, sounded like perfection. If I was his, then I was safe and protected at all times. I believed him when he said he would do anything for me. I hadn't realized how much I needed him in my life until I'd met him.

"I'm yours," I repeated. "Yours." Just because I loved the sound of it and the thought alone made my core melt with lust and... so much more. It was too early to say love. It frightened me, almost. "I'm yours, Mason."

"Mine."

He let out a groan, and I felt him grow bigger and harder inside me, if that was possible. He increased the pace and intensity, and fucked me so fast and hard, drove so deeply into me that I found I couldn't think anymore. I couldn't form one coherent sentence, so I gave up and simply gasped and moaned. When I became too loud, I covered my mouth with my hand. Above me, Mason let out little grunts and growls. His fire burned so brightly that I was surprised it hadn't set the sheets ablaze.

"I'm so close, Maya... So close..."

I nodded, since I couldn't speak. I was more than close, I was there. The second orgasm hit me so hard that I flew off the bed completely and clung to him, my body pressed to his as he held me in his arms. I felt him come inside me, and this time, it did burn. Not unpleasantly, not in a way that hurt me, but in an overwhelming, all-consuming way. Now I was certain I was his forever, because no other man would ever make me feel like this.

And all I wanted to feel was... this.

"Maya..."

He came with such power that I felt his cum shoot straight into my womb. I was covered in sweat, felt so hot that I could crawl out of my own skin, but at the same time, I felt like I was floating. My mind traveled out of my body, and for a few blissful moments, nothing mattered. Not the past, not the future. All

I knew was the present, and that Mason and I were one.

Never had I thought that sex could be life changing.

Slowly, we came down from it. Mason rolled on his side, careful not to crush me, and I snuggled against him, wanting to feel his warmth and nothing else. I felt his cum pour out of me. Curious to see what it looked like, I reached between my legs and dipped my fingers in it.

A reddish orange. I laughed. It felt like fire and looked like fire.

"What?" he asked.

"Did you know that human cum is white? I mean, sort of a transparent white. Milky, let's say."

His eyes widened. "I did not know that. Thank you for the... um... information?"

"You're welcome."

"I hope you're not too disappointed." He chuckled as he draped an arm over me.

"Not at all." I stuck a finger in my mouth and licked it with interest. "Mmm... not at all."

His eyes glowed red. "You're such a tease."

I hid my face in his neck. We stayed like that for minutes on end, just listening to each other's heartbeat.

My racing thoughts wouldn't let me rest for long, though.

"Now what?" I asked him. "After all that's happened, how do I get back to my life?"

He sighed. "One day at a time, Maya. That's all I can say. I'm sorry. But know that I am here for you. Always. You don't have to do it alone."

"Good. If I'm with you, then I can do it one day at a time."

Even though it was the middle of the day, I drifted to sleep.

MASON

My phone vibrated on the nightstand. I reached for it, trying not to wake up Maya. I frowned when I saw a text from my brother.

"Didn't want to disturb you, but the police are here."

I got out of bed and dressed in a matter of seconds. Maya cracked open an eye.

"Where are you going?"

"Go back to sleep," I said, leaning in to kiss her lips and draw the duvet over her naked form. "Everything is fine."

She nodded and yawned. My heart was beating so wildly that I was surprised she couldn't hear it. It thrummed in my ears, making me feel a little sick to my stomach. I rushed downstairs as I urged myself to calm down. I knew this was going to happen. There was nothing to be worried about. The four of us had the story straight, and there was no reason for the police to not believe us.

All the evidence at the Lockwood mansion had been destroyed. The only eyewitness who knew what had happened and could cause trouble was Victoria Lockwood, but she'd seemed relieved to finally escape. She'd told me she wanted to enjoy the little time she had just being free and doing the things she liked, and I believed her. Now I wasn't so sure. As I entered the living room, where Kara and Goliath were sitting with two policemen – one human, the other werewolf – I prayed Victoria Lockwood hadn't played me.

"Mason Stonewarden?" the wolfman asked.

I nodded and took a seat in one of the empty armchairs. Kara jumped to her feet and disappeared into the kitchen. Goliath seemed to be perfectly calm and composed, and that gave me courage.

"I am detective Cross," the wolfman said, "And this is detective Pierce. We will ask you some questions if that's alright."

"Sure. What happened, detectives?"

"You were recently hired by Dr. Vincent Lockwood. Can you tell us what your job is?"

"Certainly. He hired me as his bodyguard. I am to patrol the grounds and keep an eye out for intruders. When he goes to the city, I am to accompany him and provide security."

"I understand," Pierce said. "When did you start working for him?"

"Four days ago."

"And today you didn't go to work…?"

"He gave me the day off. Last night, he said he didn't need me, so I came to visit my brother and his family. Why? What's wrong?"

I hoped I looked and sounded clueless enough. On the inside, I was burning and having trouble keeping my fire subdued.

"His house burned down last night. Someone was driving by this morning and saw the fire from a distance. Dr. Lockwood lived quite isolated and, as you know, he didn't have any neighbors. By the time the fire was put out, it was too late. We wondered if you knew anything about it."

I shook my head. "I'm sorry. This is terrible. I was here all night." I turned to Goliath. "When did I get here? At around… ten?"

My brother nodded. "I didn't check the time, but it sounds about right. We'd just put the kids to bed."

Talking about the kids… I noticed Xavier and Nira weren't home from kindergarten. Then Kara walked out of the kitchen with a pitcher of lemonade and four glasses, placed them on the coffee table, and rushed out of the living room.

"Sorry, I have to go get the kids. Detectives, if you don't have any more questions for me…"

"Thank you for your time, Mrs. Stonewarden. You've been of great help."

She nodded and disappeared into hers and Goliath's bedroom. I trusted she was going to tell the kids exactly what to say before bringing them home. Not that I expected Cross and Pierce to question them. They were too young.

"Okay, there are just a few more details we'd like to clear up with you," Cross said.

There were footsteps upstairs, then I heard Maya descend the stairs. I tensed up for a moment. Cross and Pierce craned their necks to see who was coming, and I could tell they were on edge. When Maya appeared in the doorway, hair mussed and clothes slightly crumpled, they relaxed and gave her a smile.

"Sorry we woke you up, Miss..."

"Maya. Maya Lucas. What's going on?"

She came to sit by my side, and I wrapped my arm around her waist. Cross and Pierce exchanged a glance.

"Can you tell us who you are?"

"I'm..."

"She's my mate," I said quickly. "With my busy schedule, we try to spend as much time together as we can. Which is not easy."

"I see." Cross gave her another look, then looked at his phone.

I saw his nostrils flare. He was scenting her, trying to determine if she was, indeed, my mate. She was drenched in my smell. She'd showered before coming downstairs, but she had me in her and all over her, and Cross knew we weren't lying. Because of their unique abilities, wolfmen made skilled detectives. A lot of shapeshifters chose careers in law and order, and there were plenty who worked for Monster Security Agency, too.

For the next five minutes, the detectives asked us a few more questions, but they were small and mostly irrelevant. Seemingly satisfied, they got up, and Maya and I walked them to the door. Outside, they thanked us again and made to leave. It didn't escape me that there were two cars parked in front of my brother's house – one was theirs, the other one was a black sedan.

"Oh, one more thing," Pierce turned and pointed at us. "There's someone else who'd like to talk to you, if that's okay." He then looked at the black sedan.

My curiosity was piqued. Next to me, Maya seemed nervous.

"Sure," I said. "Whatever we can do to help."

The car door opened, and a man stepped out. He was dressed in a tailored suit. He looked young, maybe in his forties, and he had dark blond hair and piercing green eyes. He was handsome, and when he smiled, he showed off a perfect set of bright teeth.

He was human, and not a detective at all. Everything about him screamed "private, wealthy, entitled."

MAYA

The police didn't even know about me. How was that possible? It was true I'd only been missing for a week, but had my parents not reported me missing? Had they not tried to call me? What about my job? Surely, someone must have realized something had happened. I refused to think no one had noticed I'd been gone.

We walked the two detectives to the door, and all I could think about was that I wanted them to leave so I could contact my parents and my workplace. I needed to sort this out. But then the sophisticated guy in a tailored suit got out of the second car, and my attention was drawn to him.

"Hello," he said, extending a hand to Mason. "I am Dr. Malcom Harlow. I was friends with Dr. Lockwood. Do you mind if we have a word inside?"

I looked at Mason, trying to read his face. Since his face, like all of him, was made of stone, he was nearly impossible to read. But we were together now. I belonged to him, and he belonged to me, so I felt like I could tell when he was feeling uncomfortable. Like now. He also gave me the impression that he was feeling apprehensive.

He nodded, though, and invited Dr. Harlow in. In the living room, no one sat down. This was going to be quick. Goliath looked up at the new visitor, then excused himself and disappeared into the kitchen.

The fact that this man had come with the police didn't escape me. He looked wealthy and powerful – the kind of guy who had people in his pocket. Were we in trouble?

"Vincent and I met in college and became good friends," Harlow said. "We worked together on a few projects but have grown apart in the past two years. We were both busy, my work often forced me to travel, and you know how people of science are. We get obsessed with our little projects and lose touch with reality, often forget there are people around us who need us."

"I understand," Mason said. "My work is time-consuming, too. We all get a little obsessed when we love what we do."

Dr. Harlow nodded, but his eyes drifted to me. I had nothing to contribute, so I retreated to the couch. However, I felt like even though Harlow was talking to Mason, he kept glancing at me, showing more interest than it made sense for him to show. He hadn't even asked me who I was.

"I just wanted to paint a picture for you, Mr. Stonewarden. So you understand how much I cared about Vincent, even though we didn't quite keep in touch anymore. When I found out about what happened last night, I was devastated. Did you know he lived with his mother?"

I saw Mason hesitate for a moment, then he nodded and looked sad.

"Terrible," Harlow continued. "That poor woman. She was sick, too. They both died in that fire, and all I can think about is that I hadn't called Vincent in months. I didn't know what he was going through. If he was going through anything at all. He's had a hard life. So, I wanted to ask you... Since you worked for him, how did he seem to you? Did he seem okay? Was he stressed?"

"I'm afraid I can't help you," Mason said. "My relationship with my clients is cold and professional.

I like to keep it that way, so I can be efficient at my job. Dr. Lockwood hired me to be his bodyguard, so that's what I was. He didn't share any personal details with me. It is possible we would've grown closer in time, since this was supposed to be a long-term job, but four days wasn't enough for me to get to know him that well. He only shared essential information that would help me do my job, but nothing personal. I'm sorry. I truly can't help you."

Harlow nodded. He looked at me again, and to my surprise, addressed me for the first time.

"I'm sorry, Miss..."

"Maya," I said.

"You must think I'm rude. I apologize. I'm just so stricken by what happened to Vincent. Do you happen to know anything?"

I forced myself to not look at Mason. I had to do my best to seem disconnected from this whole story. The police knew I was Mason's mate, so that's why I was here. As for Lockwood, I was supposed to have no idea who he was. Certainly, I didn't know where his mansion was, and I'd just heard about him, really, since Mason wasn't supposed to share details about his clients. Not even with his family.

"I'm sorry," I said, doing my best to give him a blank stare. "I first heard his name today. What happened is simply heartbreaking. I'm so sorry for your loss."

Harlow nodded. "Thank you, Maya. It means a lot to me."

I was sure it meant nothing to him at all. There was something deeply fake about him, which confused me, because why would he be fake? Unless he was lying, and he wasn't a friend of Lockwood's. I wondered what his angle was, then. Where did his interests really lie?

"I won't take any more of your time," he said. "Thank you for your patience."

He shook hands with Mason, then Mason walked him to the door. The police had waited for Dr. Harlow, and the two cars drove away together once Harlow got into his. I stayed behind. Harlow had given me the creeps. In a way, he gave off the same vibe as Lockwood. Or maybe I just had an aversion to scientists now.

Goliath joined me in the living room.

"That was weird," he said.

"I don't believe him," I said.

"That he was friends with Lockwood?"

"Maybe he was, maybe he wasn't. I don't believe he came here because he was worried about him. He kept looking at me every five seconds."

Mason returned with Kara and the two children. That was when I realized Kara had been gone for a while. She was carrying a bag of groceries, while Mason was carrying two. Xavier and Nira threw off their shoes and backpacks in the hallway, then ran into the kitchen screaming, "Ice cream! Ice cream!"

"I thought I'd do some shopping," Kara said, smiling. "Give you guys time to finish with the police."

That had been smart of her. It was better to not involve the children if she could avoid it.

Suddenly, I felt like a burden to them. I'd come into their lives and disrupted their peace. Now they were both lying for me, a random human woman whom they'd just met a couple of hours ago. Well, maybe not random, since I was Mason's mate, but still... Everything was happening too fast, and I was asking too much of these kind, lovely people.

"Mason..." I went to him and wrapped my arms around his waist. He pulled me in, and I rested my cheek on his chest. "I want to go home. Will you take me home?"

"I don't know... I mean, yes, of course. But I don't know if it's safe."

"The police have no clue what happened to me. And that's fine. I want to put it behind me. I need to call my parents, call my work, assess the damage, come up with a story..."

"I understand." He kissed the top of my head. "I will take you home."

"Thank you."

I thanked Goliath and Kara, said goodbye to the kids, then let Mason lead me to his truck. I promised I would visit them soon, but the truth was I wanted to be alone for a while.

I dreamed about getting pizza and eating it alone in my bed while staring into space and processing everything that had happened to me. I loved being with Mason, but he had this effect on me... Whenever I was with him and we touched, he took all my pain away. He made my darkest thoughts vanish, and while I was grateful for that, as it eased my soul and my mind, I was also aware that I needed to sit with them at some point and actually process them, or I was going to end up with a lot of pent-up emotions and hidden trauma.

Being with someone who felt right was amazing. Mason was the one for me. I knew that. But I still needed to be alone with myself sometimes.

I was sure he would understand.

MASON

The neighborhood where Maya lived was quiet, with small houses and manicured lawns. It was middle-class, human exclusive, and most families had children. Maya lived in a cute house that was positively tiny for me. I pulled into the driveway, my truck so big that it occupied all the available space. Down the street, an old lady was walking her dog and two teenage girls were looking at their phones and laughing. When I got out of the truck, I could feel their eyes on me. Silence fell, and as I went to help Maya out, I was keenly aware of their stares. They were shocked to see a monster in their neighborhood.

There were no conflicts between humans and monsters. The only reason we were divided sometimes was the simple fact that we needed widely different living conditions. As a golem, I could fit into living spaces designed for humans a little more easily, but there were monsters who couldn't use human houses, or elevators, or even human beds. There were species of monsters who had to build entire neighborhoods and communities for themselves because their needs were very specific.

Golems only needed space. A lot of it, if we wanted to be comfortable. It was just that we were so tall, and wide, and heavy that human living spaces felt like tiny cages to us.

Maya produced a key from under a pot and unlocked the front door. I squeezed inside after her. I followed her into her tiny living room, where I almost bumped into her.

"Sorry," I said.

She ignored me. I found she was acting odd. She just stood in the middle of the room, staring at the couch and the coffee table. There were clothes strewn on the couch, and a few beauty products scattered around, as if she'd been in a hurry the last time she'd left the house.

"What's wrong?" I asked.

"I didn't do this."

She marched into her bedroom. Her house seemed to have only the one floor and the attic. In the bedroom, the bed and the floor were littered with clothes and shoes, and in the middle of the room, there was an open suitcase.

"Where's my other suitcase? The big one..." She looked for it for two minutes before she declared, "It's gone."

And then it dawned on me. She looked at me, and on her face, I saw the same realization I was having.

"That's why the police didn't know anything about me," she said. "Lockwood came here and made it look like I'd packed up and left. My parents probably think I went crazy or something. I need to call them. And I need to call my job."

"How can I help?"

"I... I don't know. Coffee? I need a cup of strong coffee."

I nodded and went into her diminutive kitchen. I had to be careful how I moved because it was way too easy for me to knock down things and make a mess. I heard her talk in the other room, and I popped my head in to see what was going on. She was on her laptop, and I heard her parents cry as she explained to them something about needing a break. I went back into the kitchen, not wanting to intrude. Plus, I wasn't sure she was going to tell her parents about me. First, they had to process the fact that their daughter was back, and safe, and well.

Half an hour later, she came into the kitchen and sat down at the table with a sigh. I placed a cup of hot coffee in front of her. She looked exhausted.

"I don't know if I should be mad or happy," she said. "That bastard made it look like I just up and left. He got rid of my phone and my laptop. He didn't find my old laptop, though. I had it shoved at the back of the closet, out of the way. I'm lucky it still works, otherwise this would've been a whole lot more difficult."

"How are your parents?"

"They're fine. They were worried, but it was only a week, so they were hopeful I'd turn up, eventually. When they realized my phone was shut off, they called my work, and one of my colleagues came in to check on me. She found the house this way, drew the obvious conclusion, and that was about it." She lifted the cup to her lips and looked up at me. "What do you think? As much as it sucks, all's well that ends well, right? And I really don't feel like telling anyone what happened. Lockwood's gone thanks to you and telling my story now would only get us both in trouble. Never speak ill of the dead."

"I will support you no matter what," I said.

"Thank you." She reached over and put her hand on mine. "I mean it."

I took her hand and lifted it to my lips. "I'm here for you. Whatever you need."

She got up and moved onto my lap. She was so tiny that she still had to crane her neck to look up at me.

"I'm confused about the future," she said. "I don't know how we can make it ours." She motioned at the kitchen. "So, this is me. This is where I live. I'm pretty sure I lost my job, though."

"We can take things slowly, if that's what you need," I said. In my head, however, I was already making plans. "There's one thing you must know, Maya. I will pursue the hell out of you."

She laughed and kissed me on the lips. "How about you show me now? How hard you're willing to pursue me..."

I didn't need to be told twice. I stood up and carried her to the bedroom. As I lowered her onto the bed and climbed on top of her, I was careful not to make any sudden movements. Her bed was small and not very sturdy, at least compared to the bed in my brother's house.

I started peeling off her clothes.

"Wait," she said. "I want to taste you. It's my turn."

As she pushed me onto my back and moved down my body to rest between my legs, I felt my head spinning. She undid my belt and pulled down my pants. Her fingers traced the length of my cock, and as I twitched upwards to meet her delicious touch, I closed my eyes and let my head fall onto the pillow.

The Mating Fire burned bright inside me. It was impossible to tame it.

MAYA

I wasn't delusional, I knew I couldn't give him a proper blowjob. I could barely fit the head of his cock in my mouth, and even that felt like it was going to dislodge my jaw. But I wanted to taste him. I wanted to let him know how much I wanted him, every part of him. I held his cock with both hands, rubbing it up and down as I sucked on the tip.

His liquid fire flooded my mouth. It was the lubricant that helped me adapt to his girth, and oddly enough, it sort of worked now too, because I could fit more of him into my mouth. Not too much, though. It was physically impossible. He tasted sweet, and I drank greedily, humming and moaning, urging him to give me more.

"Maya, you're driving me crazy," he murmured.

I hummed louder, knowing it would send vibrations down his length. I felt him shudder under me. His reaction made me melt with desire. My core throbbed for him, and my pussy soaked my panties and jeans. I couldn't wait to have him inside me. Had it not been for the fact that he could literally make my pussy adjust to him, it would've been impossible for us to have sex twice in one day.

I sucked the head of his cock and lapped up everything he was willing to give me. He was becoming restless. I felt his hands in my hair, and when I looked up at him, I caught him staring down at me. Our gazes met, and I grinned as I licked him like a lazy cat.

"Come here," he said, pulling me up. I let his cock slip out of my mouth and licked my lips seductively. "Ride me."

I got rid of my clothes as quickly as I could. His hips were so wide that I ended up sitting on top of him, not exactly straddling him. It was more comfortable than I'd expected. I raised my hips, and he helped me position his cock at my entrance, then I lowered myself gradually. His liquid fire shot inside me, and I felt its effects instantly. I could take him inch by inch until he was inside me completely. When I lifted myself and sat back down, all I felt was bliss. There was no pain with Mason. Despite our size difference, we fit together perfectly. It was unbelievable, but it was the best sex I'd ever had. It was the sex I always wanted to have from now on.

"My beautiful mate," he said as he grabbed my hips and guided me up and down his cock. "You're all I want. You're all I need. I will make you happy."

I leaned over him, and he sat up to meet me halfway. We kissed passionately as I bounced on top of him, faster and faster, until I felt like it was becoming overwhelming, and he had to take over and thrust upwards. I was getting closer and closer. I furrowed my brows and focused on the heat that was building in my belly. He shoved himself deep inside me. Once, twice, and the orgasm rippled through me, making me shake with the force of it. Mason held me there, his hands the only thing that kept me from collapsing. I felt his cum fill me to the brim, hot and sticky, and that coaxed a second orgasm from my tired, trembling body.

I lay on top of him, my head on his chest, and waited for my heart to calm down. It was beating so wildly that it was almost hurting me. He played with my hair and ran his hands over my bare back as the droplets of sweat that covered me from head to toe slowly evaporated.

We stayed like that for a while, maybe half an hour. I was about to fall asleep when I felt him stir underneath me. I rolled off him and onto my side, and he got up and started looking for his clothes.

"Where are you going?" I asked.

Earlier, when we'd left his brother's place, I'd been thinking about how I needed time alone, but now that he was getting ready to leave, I wasn't so sure anymore. We'd just met, and I felt like I couldn't live without him.

"If I'm going to take care of you and provide for you, then I need to get some things in my life in order." He came over to the bed and kissed me. "I'll be back later. I'll bring you a new phone, too."

"Thank you."

We kissed again, then he was gone. I stayed in bed for a while longer, but I needed to take a shower, and then I needed to get something to eat. It was getting dark outside. I didn't know what Mason had meant when he'd said he'd be back later, but I wasn't worried. He knew where I kept the spare key.

I washed myself quickly, got into my comfy house clothes, then ordered pizza and cleaned up the living room as I waited. It didn't take me long to notice that more than my phone and my laptop were missing. A bunch of clothes, two pairs of shoes, my shampoo and conditioner, and a few other beauty products. Lockwood had probably stuffed them all in my suitcase, and then thrown the suitcase into the water. Or something like that. I wasn't happy that some of my best things were missing, but I was alive and in one piece, and I'd met my soulmate. I had nothing to complain about.

The pizza came, I tipped the guy generously, then sat down and ate in front of the TV. Three slices in, I felt so tired that I couldn't keep my eyes open. I wrapped a blanket around myself and cozied up on the couch, turning down the volume and letting the 90s sitcom run in the background.

I must've been sleeping for an hour when I was woken up by a noise coming from the front door. My first thought was that Mason was back, so I pulled the blanket to my chin and dozed back off. Heavy footsteps rang through the house, which again, wasn't too suspicious, because Mason was someone one could hear from miles away. But then they rushed into the living room, and the urgency made me poke my head over the back of the couch to see what was going on.

There were two men, big and dressed in black from head to toe. Their faces were covered. I screamed and scrambled off the couch, falling and slamming my shoulder into the coffee table.

"No," I said. "No, not again."

The two men closed in on me before I could properly get up. They grabbed me, and one of them held me as the other pressed a funny-smelling cloth to my mouth and nose.

I was getting flashbacks.

A third man entered the living room. He was dressed in a tailored suit, and I recognized him immediately. Dr. Malcolm Harlow.

"Surprised?" he asked me sarcastically. "You shouldn't be, Miss Lucas. You know how valuable the blood that runs through your veins is."

I blacked out.

MASON

I saw the black sedan pull out of Maya's driveway as I was coming from the other direction. I stopped the truck and watched, allowing some distance between us, then followed it with my lights turned off. My glowing eyes helped me see in the dark. My vision wasn't as good as a shapeshifter's, but it was better than a human's. I hung back and tried to be as inconspicuous as possible, which was not an easy feat, seeing how my truck was huge. It was late, and there wasn't much traffic. With my sharp sight, I was able to follow the black sedan even when two, then three cars separated us.

Our destination seemed to be the port. When I figured it out, I felt sick to my stomach. The fire in my belly started burning, and I felt equally angry and anxious. I had to get to Maya in time, or they were going to ship her off somewhere. I knew the black sedan belonged to Dr. Malcolm Harlow. I'd just seen it a few hours ago, though the plates were different. Who else could it have been? No, I was certain it was him. And when he'd come inside my brother's house to ask me about Lockwood, he'd actually wanted to see Maya up close.

It was all crystal clear to me now. Lockwood had hired me to guard the door to the basement, not because Maya might've escaped, but because someone else might've come and taken her from him. His old friend, Harlow.

The closer we got to the port, the sparser the traffic. I hung way back. I didn't want to spook Maya's kidnappers, because I had something serious in store for them. It started with "d" and ended with "eath". I'd made a promise – to protect my mate at all times and no matter the cost. I'd turned my back for two hours, maybe less, and another bastard had kidnapped her a second time.

I saw the black sedan stop. I parked my car behind a building and got out in time to see two men carrying Maya to a shipping container. I grit my teeth and forced my fire to settle down. I had to be careful. These guys could've been armed. They most likely were. And I was too far away to save Maya if they decided to hurt her. I couldn't let them see me until it was too late for them.

A third man got out of the car. He had blond hair that shined in the moonlight. Dr. Malcolm Harlow. I hadn't spared his friend, so I wasn't going to spare him.

It looked like Maya was sedated. She didn't move and didn't make a sound. When the two men placed her in the container, walked out and locked her in, she didn't bang on the door. Harlow said something to them, then turned away and started talking on the phone.

I saw no reason to wait. I moved closer, making sure my massive frame was at least somewhat obscured by the containers lined up, waiting to be hauled onto a ship. I breathed in and out steadily, pushing my fire down, down, down. If I let it burn now, I would be like a walking torch, which would take away the advantage I had. Slowly, carefully, without a sound, I got as close as I could.

One of the guys heard me and turned, pulling out a gun. I stepped out from behind the container and stood in front of him, hands on my hips, finally letting my fire take over. The guy shot me a few times, then the other guy joined him. Nothing happened. The bullets bounced off my stone body. They weren't the right ones.

It wasn't that golems were invincible. We weren't. But it took a certain kind of metal that was treated in a certain kind of way – and magic was involved too, though some preferred to call it chemistry – to penetrate our bodies. My brother had been unlucky enough to deal with people who were prepared for him.

These guys were not prepared for anything. I hoped they were prepared to die.

I needed to move fast, because Harlow saw me, and as his men kept shooting at me, he ran to his car. I couldn't let him get away, which meant I had to get rid of his goons quick.

I let my fire rage, turning into a torch so massive and bright that half of the port became illuminated. I ran toward the two men in black, and they realized too late what was about to happen. One of them pulled off his mask, but I didn't care about his identity. I slammed into them and wrapped one arm around each, effectively setting them on fire.

My fire was powerful and all-consuming. Once I set something ablaze, there was no going back. Had the firefighters gotten to the Lockwood mansion in time, they wouldn't have been able to put out the fire. But that was not something that was common knowledge. Golems didn't share these tidbits with just anyone.

I dropped the two burning bodies and turned to Harlow, who had started the car and was driving away. I ran, and when I was close enough to the tail of the car, I took a jump and landed right in front of it. Harlow slammed into me, which smooshed the front of the car like a pancake.

He was in shock. The airbag had deployed, and he fought it while trying to get the car door to open. It was stuck. Unhurriedly, I walked to the driver's side and pulled the door out of its hinges. Harlow looked at me with wide eyes, as if he couldn't believe what was happening.

"You don't have to do this," he said. "We can talk. This is only business, nothing personal. And I'm good at doing business. Just name your price."

"My price is your life," I said as I grabbed him by the arm and pulled him out of the car.

I heard and felt his arm pop out of its socket. Harlow screamed in pain, but I didn't care. I threw him onto the ground and stood over him, my fire burning menacingly.

"What were you going to do with Maya?" I asked.

"Nothing. She's free to go. You can take her. I'll pay you whatever you want, and you can start a life together. How would you like that?"

"I don't need your dirty money."

It occurred to me he probably knew why I'd agreed to work for Lockwood. He knew I wasn't in a great financial situation. What he didn't know was that I was done letting that control me, dictate what my values were.

"Something else, then," he said. "What do you want?"

I growled at him.

"Do you want to be the head of the MSA branch here in the city? I can do that for you. Easily. Just say the word."

He had everyone in his pocket, didn't he? My boss, too. Did that mean Lockwood had had the same influence?

"Stop talking bullshit and tell me what I want to know," I said. "What were you going to do with Maya?"

He let out a sigh and let his head hit the pavement. I crouched over him, grabbed him by his tailored shirt, and pulled him to a standing position.

"Now, Harlow."

"Her blood is valuable. Coming across people like her is rare. Not a vampire, not a dhampir, but just enough healing properties in her blood that it can cure the most horrible diseases. Temporarily. Of course, for a permanent solution, pure vampire blood is recommended, but that comes with giving up one's humanity and mortality. I hear being immortal is not as romantic as many of us might think."

"So?"

"I was going to sell her on the black market."

"Is this what you did to Lockwood's other victims?"

"Just the last two before Maya. The others, he got rid of them himself. He either couldn't control them and had to cut his losses, or they found a way to... well... off themselves. That basement of his is not exactly a luxury hotel room. I told him he should keep them in better conditions, but he wanted to hide them from his mother. That woman was his undoing. He was obsessed with keeping her alive and keeping her human. I couldn't relate. I never knew my mother. Had it not been for Victoria, Vincent would've joined me in this business and made tons of money. Real money."

"So, you were friends, you worked together, and you betrayed him."

"We met in college, yes. I didn't lie about that. He wanted to find a cure for his mother's cancer, and we started the project together. It was trial and error for a long time, but then we got it right. The only problem was that we needed an endless supply of fresh blood. The right blood. I had a stronger stomach than him, at least in the beginning. After that, he surpassed me and became capable of pretty gruesome things. I brought our first victim. It was a boy. We kept working together for a while, but at some point, it wasn't as satisfying to me. We were doing all this work to help his mother when there were so many others who needed help. We had what they needed, and they had money. It was a fair exchange. Vincent refused to get into the business, so I left. But it was hard to find people with the right type of blood. Too much work. At some point, I figured it was easier to let Vincent find them, and when he wasn't on his guard, swoop in and grab them."

"I knew it," I said. "He hired me to protect Maya from you."

"And what a great job you're doing."

He grinned, and I knew he was going to negotiate with me again. This guy never gave up.

"I will never touch her again, I promise," he said. "When I saw her with you at your brother's house, I should've known this would never work. I was blinded by greed. I have a buyer in Europe, and Vincent took his sweet time finding Maya after the last one. I understand I was wrong, and my greed and rush to satisfy my buyer got me in this mess."

"You talk a lot, did you know that?"

"Well, you asked me to talk." He spread his arms wide, as if to show that he was just being cooperative. "I can give you money, and I can make you head of the MSA branch. You would be set for life."

"No, I'm good." He blanched, and I took a moment to delight in it. "Who else knows about Maya?"

He shook his head. "No one."

"Why would I believe you?"

"It's the truth. Vincent did all the research on her. I didn't even see her file. He has files on all his victims. But I don't care for the details, I just want the blood."

I nodded. I hoped he was telling the truth, but there was no way to know for sure, and I would have to live with it. It just meant I would have to protect my mate twenty-four-seven. I could do that. It was an honor for me to act as her personal bodyguard.

I let my fire burn bright again.

Harlow's eyes widened. As I stood over him, his whole body seemed to be aglow.

"I said the wrong thing," he rushed to apologize. "Made it sound like she's an object. She's not."

"Shut up."

I directed my flames at him. He tried to crawl away, but his clothes and hair were on fire. His screams were music to my ears.

I waited for the fire to consume him until only ashes and bones were left, then went to check on the other two idiots who'd made the mistake of crossing me. Ashes and bones. That was what happened when someone dared to lay a finger on my fated mate. I left no evidence behind. The police would identify them by their dental records, but they wouldn't be able to tell what had happened to them, how they'd ended up burned to nothing.

I found the key to the container Maya was in. I saved her a second time. Not that it bothered me, but I really hoped this was the last time.

MAYA

I couldn't tell if I had my eyes open or not. It was that dark. I touched my face, pressed my fingers to my temple, and groaned. Great. I had a headache. I reached my hand behind my head and felt around. There was the old wound, but it was nearly healed. My memory was intact, too. At least this time, I hadn't hit my head and gotten a concussion. All in all, it was progress. I was getting better at being kidnapped.

But where was I?

I felt around the space. The floor was cold, made of metal. It seemed to be cramped, and there wasn't a lot of air in here. My hands and feet were freezing. I couldn't find a light switch. I checked my pockets and then remembered I didn't have a phone. Mason had said he'd bring me one.

Mason. He was going to have a surprise when he got back to my house.

As I saw it, I had two options. Bang on the walls of this box Harlow had put me in and scream my head off or wait silently and patiently for Mason to find me. Because I knew he would find me. He'd promised to protect me, and he'd done it once. He would do it again. I didn't know how, but he would figure out where I was and come save me. It was odd to think this way... I'd been kidnapped a second time in the span of one week, I was trapped once again with no way out, and somehow... I felt calm.

I turned my back to the wall and slid down, hugging my knees to my chest. From experience, I knew that if I banged on the door and made noise, nothing would happen. These people had ways of making sure that no one would hear me. At least I wasn't cuffed or tied up. But this box was worse than Lockwood's basement, because he'd at least given me a mattress and a bucket. Oh, there had been a chair, too. Furniture!

I focused on my breathing and listened to the silence. It didn't last long. Soon, I heard noises outside. Gunshots, people screaming, heavy footsteps. Mason was here. He had to be. I jumped to my feet and pressed myself to the door – or what

I thought was the door. I listened closely and heard voices. Mason's voice carried over. He was talking in a low, menacing tone. I couldn't understand the words, but it sounded like he was interrogating someone.

My first instinct was to call him, now that I knew he was here, let him know where I was. But then I realized he had everything under control. I waited, feeling relieved that I didn't have to do anything, that I didn't have to make strategies and try to get myself out of this situation, which, by the way, I hadn't created. It wasn't my fault my ancestor was a damn vampire. It wasn't my fault my blood had healing properties. If it was so extraordinary, why hadn't I healed from my concussion faster? It seemed unfair that something that literally ran through my body could help others, but never me.

There was more screaming, and then silence. Heavy footsteps came closer and closer, and I moved away from the door. I heard a key turn in the lock. The door opened, and I had to shield my eyes from the brightness that surrounded Mason. His fire burned through him, flames spilling through the cracks in his skin.

"Maya," he said.

"I knew you'd find me," I said.

His fire tamed a little, and I threw myself into his arms. He held me for minutes on end as I clung to him, whispering in his ear to never let me go. He picked me up, and I wrapped my legs around his waist. Or tried to. The heat of his body seeped into my bones. My soul was full of him, and my mind was at ease, knowing that I was safe. Knowing that since I was Mason's mate, I was always safe, and he would always find me and rescue me.

"It was Harlow," I said. "He wanted the same thing Lockwood did. My blood."

"Yes. Now he doesn't want anything because he's no more. You don't have to worry about him."

I let go of Mason and looked around me. We were at the port. Harlow and his men had put me in a container. I shuddered. What were they going to do to me? Ship me off to... where?

Mason saw all these questions in my eyes.

"Europe," he said. "He had a buyer."

"What?!"

"Apparently, people like you have great value on the black market."

I shook my head. "Harlow was worse than Lockwood."

"I'd say they were equally bad."

I noticed something on the ground and went to see what it was. Mason followed me, but didn't stop me. When I saw the two burned bodies, I covered my mouth with my hands. A few feet away, there was a third one.

"You killed them," I said.

Mason studied my profile. "Are you upset about that?"

I thought for a moment, then shook my head. "No. What they were going to do to me, they surely did to many before me. They got what they deserved."

He pulled me to him for a second, kissed the top of my head, then kneeled before me, right there, on the pier.

"Maya, I want to spend my life with you. I love you."

His eyes glowed with so much emotion that tears gathered in my own eyes. Mason had done this for me. He'd turned three people to ashes, not because he wanted to and enjoyed doing it, but because they'd dared to touch me.

"I love you, too," I said.

"I want you to move in with me. I went to talk to my brother, and there's a house I can buy down the street from him. You will be safe there, in a neighborhood of golems. No one will dare to even look at you the wrong way."

"What about my job?"

"You vanished for a week, one of your colleagues went to check on you and concluded you'd run away. They don't appreciate you. They don't care. I will provide for you, my love. If you want to work, I will help you find something. I'm sure Kara has ideas. But you don't have to work, if you don't want to."

"I like working with children," I said.

"There's a kindergarten and a school. I think either of them could use a human teacher, since some of the kids are hybrids."

I smiled. He took my hands in his and looked deep into my eyes.

"Maya Lucas, will you marry me?"

My jaw dropped. Asking me to move in with him was one thing, but asking me to marry him... Well, I guess it made sense. We were soulmates. Why wait?

"Yes. I will marry you, Mason Stonewarden."

With him on his knees, we were finally on the same level. I cupped his face with my hands and kissed him passionately. It didn't escape me he'd chosen to ask me to marry him among the ashes of my enemies. One might've said it was quite romantic.

"I'll take you home," he said. "And this time, I won't let you out of my sight."

I chuckled. "That works for me."

As we made our way to his truck, I threw one last glance at the shape that used to be Dr. Malcolm Harlow.

"What about the police? Will they not investigate?"

"They will, but who cares? They won't be able to tell what happened here. There are no cameras. I checked. That's a hundred percent courtesy of Harlow, who was doing black market business here."

"But the detectives we talked to today..."

"They were on his payroll, I'm sure. They'll either be sad their cash cow died, or they will be glad to finally be rid of him. I don't think they'll bother us. Either way, they have no evidence."

"Because you don't leave any."

"Not a single clue, no."

I laughed as he helped me into his truck. "I like the way you operate. You're efficient."

"That's what makes me a great asset. Too bad I don't have a job."

That made me pause. It had come out of nowhere, and I would've expected him to be upset about it, but as he started the truck, it looked to me like he was feeling upbeat and optimistic.

He noticed my staring and laughed. "Don't worry. I'm getting it back."

"How?"

"Let's say that our adventures with mad scientists and black-market businessmen these past few days have revealed information that I can leverage. Don't worry about a thing, my love. I've got it all under control."

I believed him, and as we drove away and left the port behind, I relaxed in the certainty that Mason knew what was best for us. I like his idea of moving to his brother's neighborhood. Kara and I would become best friends, and I would never be on my own again.

People who had loving families and true friends didn't get kidnapped.

Epilogue

Mason

I hadn't thought we'd have such a blast moving in together, but Maya was so excited about the new house, so impressed with how spacious it was, that she swept me up in her great mood, and now I caught myself humming and whistling random songs she listened to every day as I worked in our backyard or assembled furniture with the invaluable help of my niece and nephew. She redecorated every room, leaving the kitchen for last. Today, we'd been shopping since morning, and the truck was loaded.

"We need one more thing," she said as she jumped into the passenger's seat. She'd figured out how to get into my tank of a truck without my help and loved showing off. "Curtains."

"What's wrong with the old ones?"

"For one, they're Kara's. I'm grateful she lent them to us so we could have privacy while we figured things out, but I don't want to abuse her generosity. Plus, they're blue. Our house is all in shades of yellow and orange now."

"All right, curtains it is!"

I pulled out of the parking lot. The store we needed was across the city, which meant this was a good opportunity to do something I'd been meaning to do for a while.

"Do you mind if we make a quick stop? There's something I need to take care of."

She eyed me suspiciously, but then smiled and shrugged. "Sure, we're in no rush."

I loved how she trusted me. Two days after we'd moved into our new home, she pulled me aside as Xavier and Nira ran from one room to another, yelling and laughing, kissed me deeply, and told me she loved not having to worry about a thing. She thanked me for making all the decisions about the move, and that she'd never felt so relaxed in her life.

Her words made me feel like a superhero.

I hadn't told her I'd had to take out a loan from the bank to afford the house, nor that I hadn't yet talked to my boss about getting my job back. I had a feeling she knew all this, but still trusted me to sort it out. And that was what I was going to do because it was my job. My mate deserved to live a life of peace and joy, and not have to think about our finances.

The truth was that when I met her, I wasn't ready for a mate. This past year, with my brother's health and financial issues, I'd been so focused on him and his family that I hadn't paid attention to my own life. Not that I was poor by any stretch, but the money I'd set aside wasn't enough for the lifestyle I wanted to provide for Maya and our future children.

I stopped in front of the Monster Security Agency headquarters and turned to Maya.

"I won't be long."

"Okay."

I kissed her, and she bit my lip playfully.

I got out of the truck, straightened my back, and squared my shoulders. In my hand, I had the file I'd been meaning to show my boss, but hadn't yet had the chance. I'd been distracted by the move, but it was time. Today was a good day for this. Enough time had passed from the incidents with Lockwood and Harlow, and I was calmer now. Composed. Had I approached Taros Mammon right after, I didn't think I would've managed to keep my anger in check.

I took the elevator to the top floor. Because of my massive frame, no one got in with me. The doors opened, and I stepped into the space that was so familiar to me. I nodded at some of my colleagues, and I could see they were intrigued as to why I was here. My boss's secretary wasn't pleased when I told her that no, I didn't have an appointment, but I was going to go in anyway.

"Sorry, I couldn't stop him," she told Taros when I barged into his office without as much as a knock.

My boss let out a sigh, then waved me in. "It's okay. Close the door, please." Then to me, "What can I do for you, Mason? Once again, you messed up. I give you a second chance, and what happens? Oh, the client bursts up in flames. Don't tell me it wasn't you because I won't believe it."

"If you know it was me, why didn't you tell the police?"

He shrugged. "It wouldn't look good for the MSA, would it?"

I nodded. "That, and Vincent Lockwood was a heartless bastard and got what was coming to him. He was a pain in your behind, wasn't he?"

Taros cocked his head to the side. His eyes glowed with hell fire, and when he exhaled, tendrils of smoke wafted through the air.

I sat down and threw the file onto his desk. I'd gotten it from Lockwood's study when I'd taken Maya's file. I'd kept it to myself, needing time to decide what to do with it.

Taros eyed it suspiciously.

"Open it," I said. "It's all in there."

"What is?"

He pulled the file toward him and scanned the first few pages. His expression changed, his jaw tightening.

"You were friends with Dr. Vincent Lockwood. You knew exactly what he was doing and why he needed a bodyguard."

"As long as the clients pay, I don't care about the business they conduct," he said.

"You also knew about Dr. Malcom Harlow, didn't you? Of course you did. You and these two bastards used to go to the same tennis club."

He closed the file, crossed his fingers on top of it, and looked me in the eye.

"What do you want, Mason?"

"What's rightfully mine. My job back."

He nodded. "Done." A beat, and then he added, "How about a ten percent pay raise? But I never want to hear about this again."

I thought for a second. He was buying me with the pay raise. I needed it, though, and no matter what he said or thought, I was good at my job. Maya could confirm.

"Sounds good," I said.

"Deal."

He extended his hand, and after I stared at it for a moment, we shook. He placed the file in one of his drawers, then asked me if I wanted a cup of coffee. Suddenly, he was being very friendly. I didn't like him. I didn't hate him, but I wasn't going to have coffee with him. I knew he wasn't a bad guy, just someone who looked the other way when shady things happened around him. I'd exaggerated when I'd said he'd been friends with Lockwood and Harlow. Yes, they used to go to the same tennis club, but it was more like Lockwood and Harlow had had him cornered all this time. With what, I didn't know. Taros hadn't corrected me, though, which meant I was right and, in fact, he was glad they were gone.

"I have someone waiting for me," I said and got up.

My boss got up and walked me to the door. That was new.

"I'll let you know when work comes in," he said.

"You do that."

I hurried to give Maya the good news. She was waiting for me in the truck, absorbed by her phone. When I got in, she shoved the phone in my face and made me check out a dozen curtains that looked all the same to me. Apparently, they were different colors, I just couldn't see it.

"Okay, okay, here we go," I said, laughing. "Next up, the curtain store."

"How was it?" she asked, her voice serious. "Did you talk to your boss?"

"Yes. He gave me my job back. And a pay raise."

She grinned at me. "As he should."

I shook my head. "You know too much for your own good."

"Did you think I wasn't aware of that second file? Sorry, Mason, but you don't hide your things well."

"So, you read it?"

"I paged through it. It's a corrupted world we live in."

"Tale as old as time," I said.

"I guess. But you'll take care of me, right?"

She grinned at me, and I reached over and squeezed her thigh. I would've kissed her, but I needed to keep my eyes on the road.

"It's my life's mission," I said.

"Awesome! You're very good at your job, you know."

I laughed. "I was just thinking that."

She punched me playfully in the shoulder, then pretended she'd bruised her knuckles. I rolled my eyes, and she laughed.

"Let's see how good you are at picking out curtains," she said.

I let out a fake groan. I loved doing this with her, and she knew it.

Epilogue
Maya

Kara helped me put on the white bodice and laced it in the back. I stood straight, unmoving, looking at myself in the full-length mirror. The dress was so perfect that I was afraid to do anything in it, walking and sitting included. Mason hadn't seen it yet. I'd told him it was bad luck for the groom to see the bride before the wedding – a human tradition. Kara had supported me, though she confessed she hadn't respected it herself on the day of her wedding.

"All done," she said, straightening her back and looking at me. "Beautiful. Now for the veil."

She placed a tiara on my head and attached the veil with expert fingers. My long, dark hair was gathered up in a bun for the first time in years, and I was wearing light makeup, tiny pearls in my earlobes, and a string of pearls around my neck. On my finger – a gorgeous diamond ring that caught the light in all the right ways. Mason had gifted me all of it – the jewelry and the wedding dress. For the dress, he'd given me his card and sent me shopping with Kara and the kids. I could get used to this life, was all I could say.

"Ready?"

Our eyes met in the mirror, and I nodded. Someone knocked on the door, and Kara went to open it. It was my mother.

"Your father is waiting outside," she said. "I just wanted to see you."

We hugged, and she wiped a tear from the corner of her eye.

"I'm so glad you're here," I said. "Thank you. It means a lot to me."

It had been hard to convince my parents to come to my wedding. When I broke it out to them that I was in love with a golem, they nearly had a heart attack. In my defense, I did ask them to sit down when I video called them and did small talk before telling them about Mason and motioning for him to step in front of the camera. Their first reaction was speechlessness, then my dad reached over my mom's shoulder and ended the call. I gave them a few minutes to recover, called them again, and I had to send Mason away so he wouldn't have to witness my parents' meltdown.

This was a month ago. They were feeling better about the whole thing now, and they were here. Kara had helped a lot. Seeing her so happy with Goliath and seeing their beautiful hybrid children had been eye-opening for my parents. Now they were excited for me to start my life as a married woman.

Hand in hand, we walked out of the room, where my father was waiting. We were having the ceremony and the party in our backyard. The thing with golem properties was that they were so big that they felt luxurious. I was thrilled to bond my fate to Mason's in our own home, with our families and friends as witnesses. We'd invited all our neighbors, and their children, hybrid or not, were running around, giggling and stealing cookies. Xavier and Nira were having the time of their lives.

The officiant was an old golem woman. Mason was waiting for me next to her. Goliath was by his side, and when the guests noticed me and my father, they took their seats and fell silent. Piano music started playing, and my father led me between the two rows of chairs.

Mason couldn't take his eyes off me, and I couldn't take my eyes off him. He looked so powerful and handsome in his tailored suit. As I approached him slowly, I saw the awe in his glowing orbs. Through the cracks in his skin, I could see the Mating Fire burn brightly. He kept it subdued, so as not to freak out our human guests, and by that, I meant my parents. They were incapable of understanding how Mason's fire worked. To be fair, I didn't quite get it myself, but I knew he would never burn me to a crisp, like my father insisted on warning me every few days.

Alas, things weren't perfect, but we were making progress. In time, my parents would have to accept this relationship was right for me, and Mason was more than right for me – he was the only one.

We stopped in front of the officiant, and my father kissed me on both cheeks. He then patted Mason on the back, and Mason stepped next to me.

"You're beautiful, Maya. You look like a queen. My queen."

I blushed. "You're not too bad yourself." I wanted to tell him he was my king, but for some reason, the thought of saying that out loud made me blush even harder. Maybe it was better to leave it for the bedroom.

The ceremony started, and I could barely focus on the officiant's words. I was so overwhelmed with emotion that my head was spinning, and I felt jitters in my stomach. I wondered if that was what Mason felt when the Mating Fire took over. When it was time to say our vows, I stumbled on my words. I had to take a deep breath and ground myself by looking into Mason's eyes. He smiled at me and squeezed my hand, and that gave me power.

There were many things I loved about him, and that was one of them – with him, I felt powerful. Safe and cared for, and like I could do whatever I set my mind to.

He'd been right about the kindergarten needing a human teacher. I went to an interview, got the job, and I couldn't wait to start working there next week. I was going to be Xavier's and Nira's teacher. They were just as stoked as I was.

My future looked great. As Mason said his vows, the understanding that this was true happiness took over, and I couldn't stop smiling. A tear tumbled down my cheek, and I didn't stop it. Mason saw it, frowned, and wiped it with the tip of his finger.

"You may kiss the bride," the officiant said.

He leaned in, I lifted myself on my tippy toes... He wrapped his arms around my waist, I clung to his neck... Our lips crashed, and I tasted his fire, breathed it in, let it consume me.

Applause and cheers exploded, but it was as if they were far away. Mason and I were in our own world, an impenetrable bubble where all that mattered was our love for each other.

We were one, and our story was just beginning.

Monster Security Agency